Mills & Boon Classics

A chance to read and collect some of the best-loved novels from Mills & Boon – the world's largest publisher of romantic fiction.

Every month, four titles by favourite Mills & Boon authors will be re-published in the *Classics* series.

A list of other titles in the *Classics* series can be found at the end of this oook.

Essie Summers

NEW ZEALAND INHERITANCE

MILLS & BOON LIMITED
LONDON · TORONTO

First published 1957
Paperback edition published 1965 under the title
Heatherleigh
This edition 1975

This edition © Essie Summers 1975

ISBN 0 263 71803 4

Made and Printed in Great Britain by
C. Nicholls & Company Ltd
The Philips Park Press, Manchester

CHAPTER ONE

ROBERTA had thought it a pity when she had to leave the car in Oamaru for repairs, but now she was glad to be approaching the ancestral home on foot. If she had driven, she might have missed the full beauty of the lane.

It was tree-lined, and dappled with shadow, sweet with birdsong, and the haunt of bees. The scent of wild violets rose from under the silver birches, and at the end of the lane a ribbon of daffodils ran by the side of the path. and disappeared under the leafy hedge to spread unconfined throughout the field beyond. A little bit of England here in New Zealand.

It had been autumn when Roberta had last seen Heatherleigh, an autumn thirteen years before, when she had been a child of twelve. These green hedges had been rose-red with hawthorn berries, the red oaks and sycamores had stood out against the sombre pines like torches lit for burning, and the orchard over to the west, that was now a fairyland of blossom, had been a tempting place where greengages and peaches and apples had hung nectar-sweet on laden boughs.

The month that Roberta had spent here then had been a memorable one, sandwiched in between a trip to Sydney, and one to India, an oasis of deep-rooted and stable things in a world that even to a twelve-year-old had seemed a succession of kaleidoscopic changes.

It had been a colourful world, interesting and vivid, but one tired, even of change. Yet Mother had loved it – Mother, who till she married an artist with restless feet had known nothing but the comfort and solidity of Heatherleigh.

Roberta paused for a moment at the great drive entrance that swept in over wide cattle-stops, and drew a deep breath. Then she picked up her small case again and trudged over the rails. A bend in the drive brought her in full view of the house

. . . so often in strange corners of the earth she had tried to conjure up for herself a picture of it all, and had failed, yet now she found herself thinking: of course!

It stood against a background of smooth green hills and dark pines, a widespread, gracious house with tall chimney-stacks and gabled roofs. Built of white Oamaru stone, weathered by years of sun and wind and rain into a harmonious grey, it faced the sunny New Zealand north.

Creepers clung lovingly about it, and rioted where they would, virginia creeper, clematis, morning glory, wistaria; and beside a window, a great espaliered apricot tree spread its bloomy branches. .

As Roberta came near she noticed a curl of smoke wreathing from a chimney, and her heart knocked against her side. She checked her pace without meaning to, and her eyes were drawn up a hill that reared high beyond the house to the right. A white ribbon of track curved up it, and there, at the summit, was a rider on a chestnut mare. He waited there, like a bronze statue, looking down on the scene below.

Roberta had seen him pause like that many times before, silent, brooding, watchful. She had laughed with George about it, and dubbed him The Hawk. They had had other nicknames for him too . . . Leatherface, and Eagle-eyes, from the way he seemed to be able to gaze into the sun. No doubt they had been impertinent brats. Marie had said so, from the superiority of her three years' seniority.

But then you couldn't imagine Marie ever using nick-names. Even after all these years Roberta could still hear Marie saying "Muir?" with that light, caressing note she used for all men, from the cowhands to the minister of the little kirk.

Yet Muir had been stern with them all, in a fashion beyond his years, this young shepherd on her grandfather's estate, but kindly too, in a dour Scots way. Roberta felt a rush of gladness that, in this at least, Heatherleigh had not altered.

As she walked on up the steps of the wide front porch the

rider suddenly came to life, wheeled his mount around, and galloped off along the skyline.

Roberta wondered if her grandfather would be the same stiffnecked old autocrat he had always been. She hadn't long to wonder. As she came to the open door there was a low growl, and sound of an inside door opening, then her grandfather arrived in the aperture, a short riding crop hooked into the collar of a thickset brindled bull terrier. There had always been bull terriers at Heatherleigh.

Robert Heatherleigh was still a tall, massive figure, but his great shoulders were stooped now, and his progress not as swift as of yore.

He peered at her uncertainly for a moment, a small figure of a girl, well knit, and holding herself with an air that somehow suggested a sturdy will; a girl with eyes that were neither green nor brown, and with honey-coloured hair that swept softly back from a broad brow and fell about her ears in a shining bell.

Before she could say "Hullo, Grandfather," he spoke.

"It's Roberta!" he said.

She had expected a brusque "Humph! So it's you, is it, after all these years!" so she was rather disconcerted to see moisture dim the old blue eyes. Then Roberta did the only thing possible, stepped close, put up her young strong arms, and kissed him.

How strange, when one had steeled oneself for reproaches, to find only gladness and welcome.

"Come awa' in, lassie, to the fire," her grandfather said, and led the way across the great hall to where on the wide hearth *manuka* logs lay smouldering. The bull terrier followed, sniffing at Roberta's ankles.

There were the inevitable questions and answers. . . . "I've come down from Auckland. . . I've had a flat there for the last six months. . . . Father died a year ago, in Sydney. . . ."

The old man lifted a blackened kettle from the hearth on to the fire.

"When that boils I'll make you a cup of tea."

7

"*You'll* make it? Why?"

He smiled tolerantly.

"We've no maids now. Can't get 'em. They all want to live closer to town than this. Old Donald and I have to manage as best we can ourselves these days. Mrs. Donald died three years ago. It's hard enough to get housekeepers in this country for a seven-roomed city house, much less a great barn of a place like this. We've shut up most of the rooms . . . and one of the shepherds' wives gives us two days a week. Donald is failing, so he rests every afternoon now. When the tea is ready, I'll call him to have a cup with us."

Roberta couldn't believe it – she had always thought of Heatherleigh as a place that would never change. She thought of rosy-faced Mrs. Donald, queen of her own kingdom, issuing orders to the gardener who looked after the kitchen garden, running the house with dignity and order, bustling the countless maids about.

Now Roberta could notice the dust on the guns over the mantel, the cobwebs in the corners, the dinginess of the loose covers, the indescribable air of a room that lacks a woman's hand. She swallowed a lump in her throat.

She went out with her grandfather, walking slowly to suit his pace, to the huge kitchen, bare and deserted, and watched as he cut slices of bought fruit cake and arranged grocer's biscuits on a plate. The larder had a damp, mouldy smell. In silence she picked up the tray and walked back to the other room.

"I'll go to tell Donald," said Grandfather. "If he's surprised in his dressing-gown he's put out. He likes to pretend everything is as it used to be, so I just humour him."

Roberta was speechless. Just humour him! Could this be Grandy?

Presently they returned, Donald shuffling in slippers that seemed to have grown too big for him, but in perfectly pressed trousers and an immaculate alpaca jacket.

He wrung Roberta's hand in evident emotion. "It's good to see you back," he said. He glanced at the tray.

"Tck! Tck!" There was all reproach in the sound. He lifted

8

it away, pulled open a drawer in a small table, and took out a spotless white linen and lace cloth. He shook it out over the table, casting a disapproving glance at his master, and, taking away the kitchen cups, went to a three-cornered cabinet in a corner, and produced two fragile cups and saucers.

Robert Heatherleigh said firmly: "Now, Donald, this is an occasion . . . my granddaughter's return, so you must drink your tea with us."

"Mphmm!" said the old man, handing Roberta the sugar basin with a hand that trembled. He took the basin from her and sat down on a chair a little back from the table, as if conceding so much, but not all, to the relaxed conventions of the day.

"I saw Muir Buchanan on the top of the hill," said Roberta. "So he's still here too."

Robert Heatherleigh nodded. "I don't know what we'd do without him."

Roberta was glad. It would be fun to meet Muir again. She wondered if he would remember the day he had spanked her and George for falling into the Pool of Darkness where they had been warned not to go. Roberta had tingled for an hour afterwards.

Of course there were other things to remember too. . . . Muir teaching them to ride, inflexible, but encouraging; teaching them to fish; sitting patiently and playing Ludo and Snakes and Ladders with them in his rooms over the stables. It must have been boring for a lad of twenty.

At that, there was a step on the porch, and a tall figure blocked out the light for a moment. Roberta turned. Here at last was someone who hadn't changed so cruelly . . . indeed he didn't look much older than she remembered him — but of course at twelve, twenty seems much older than thirty-three to twenty-five.

He nodded casually to Robert and Donald, then to Roberta in a tone that held no hint of surprise, that indeed was completely expressionless.

"Hullo, Roberta. I saw you from the hill."

Roberta couldn't have explained why she felt as if a

9

douche of cold water had suddenly descended upon her. Why should she care, anyway, if her grandfather's shepherd expressed no pleasure at seeing her?

But . . . it hurt. They had been such pals those long years ago. She thought of the picnics, the working parties when Muir had so patiently allowed her and George to help with odd jobs in the shearing sheds, had taught them to groom the horses, polish the harness, muck out the cowsheds. Of course, it wouldn't have meant so much to Muir . . . she and George had just been a pair of kids, nuisances probably, and four weeks wasn't much out of a lifetime.

Roberta showed none of this outwardly. She chatted away easily, with the assurance acquired in social contacts in the cities of the world.

Muir sat down, uninvited, on an arm of a chair, seized one of the kitchen cups Donald had despised, and poured himself a cup of tea.

H'm, thought Roberta, in thirteen years Muir Buchanan has certainly established himself as one of the family! She was immediately ashamed of the snobbish thought.

The telephone rang in the study. Old Donald shuffled off to answer it. He came back to call old Robert to the instrument, and went away himself, taking the tea tray with him.

Muir finished his cup of tea in silence, then rose and placed his empty cup on the mantelshelf. He turned and stood with his back to the fire, a tall, lean figure, in riding breeches, his hawklike gaze fixed upon Roberta's upturned face.

She blinked a little, uncertainly.

"How long are you here for, Roberta?"

She said quietly, without resentment, "I don't know – yet."

There was a curl to Muir's lip as he asked: "You heard of your grandfather's illness some weeks ago, I suppose?"

Her eyes were clear and guileless as she answered with a puzzled inflection: "No . . . I didn't know he'd been ill – but I thought I would like to see him. After all, he's nearly eighty."

"Exactly," he said dryly.

Something in his tone, a hint of contempt, made Roberta flush a little.

She said quickly: "I couldn't come before, Muir."

"Couldn't you?" The tone carried disbelief.

Roberta looked down and said nothing. If Muir behaved like this, then she wouldn't explain the multitude of things that had hindered her. Muir seemed the only one unchanged outwardly . . . inwardly he wasn't even the same person.

A current of antagonism flowed between them.

"Did you know George was back, too?" There was still that mocking glint in his eyes, still the sting of something in the commonplace words.

Roberta rose eagerly.

"George? . . . but how lovely . . . where is he?"

Muir Buchanan shook his head.

"He's in Dunedin for a couple of days on business. He's been here some time. *He* knew about your grandfather's illness all right."

Roberta ignored whatever Muir's emphasis might mean.

"I've never seen George once in all these years. We were in Perth for a visit once, but he was away in Queensland. That was five years ago. We saw his mother. I believe she died soon after. How is George?"

"Pretty well. He's very changed, though . . . in some ways."

Roberta said sombrely: "We've all changed, Muir."

Their eyes met, considering that. Muir's expression didn't alter. His face had always been hard to read, but when he spoke again, the harshness had gone from his voice.

"Marie came. As soon as she heard your grandfather was out of hospital, she came down and asked if she could nurse him. She was here six weeks, then went back to Wellington."

Marie! Nursing! It didn't sound at all like the Marie she had known years ago. Marie had never been given to impulsive kindnesses. There had always been a motive behind her acts. Could it have been an excuse to be near Muir?

Angry with herself, Roberta pushed the ungenerous thought aside. Besides, Marie would probably be married by

11

now. She opened her lips to ask, but at that moment there was a commotion outside, and in shot a sturdy boy of perhaps ten, with fair, thick hair, cut in a straight fringe across his forehead, and a snubby nose and blue eyes.

"I say – my pony, she has her hoof all tangled up in barbed wire . . . hurry!"

"Right, son," said Muir, and was across the width of the hall to the door, in seconds.

Roberta called impulsively: "Could I help, Muir?"

He turned at the open doorway and shook his head.

"No, thanks," he said, with a courtesy that dispelled the camaraderie that had once existed between them. "Hank and I can manage."

Roberta sat on, a stranger in her grandfather's house.

Roberta and her grandfather were having their dinner, a meal that consisted of watery mince with a ring of fast-congealing fat about it, a large helping of insufficiently cooked spring cabbage, tough and dark, and lumpy potatoes that would have been vastly improved by being well beaten and having butter and milk added.

"Donald is a very indifferent cook, I'm afraid," said her grandfather apologetically, "but he pays as much attention as ever to the silver."

True enough . . . the fine old silver and crystal shone as of yore when Mrs. Donald had served those appetising and artistic meals.

"Would he mind if I took over the cooking while I'm here?" asked Roberta.

"*Can* you cook?"

"Moderately well, Grandfather."

"No, Donald wouldn't mind. He hates the cooking. One of the shepherds' wives cooks us a good roast dinner every Saturday. Donald relinquishes the pots and pans to her very gladly."

That reminded her.

"Did Muir marry an American, Grandy? I noticed he called his little boy Hank. I got such a surprise . . . I'd expect

12

Muir Buchanan's son to be called Hamish, or Angus, or something equally Scots ... never Hank!"

Old Robert sat back and chuckled.

"Hank – it's spelt H-e-n-k, by the way – isn't American, it's Dutch. And he's not Muir's son. I've got a Dutch couple, the van Wyngens, living on the Lea Farm. It's not a large house and there are five other children in the family. Henk was the orphaned nephew of Mrs. Van Wyngen, so he emigrated from Holland with them. They're wonderful workers. Henk worships Muir, and so Muir took him to live with him."

"Over the stables?"

Her grandfather looked surprised.

"Oh, no. Muir has had his own farm, Buchanan, this last ten years or more. He bought that piece of land over the bridge past the Haughs' from me. He built there, and farms it himself, but still oversees most of my labourers."

Roberta said nothing, but thought that that explained Muir's changed status. She nodded and said briskly:

"When dinner is over, I'll see Donald about my taking over the cooking. I'll have a look around the kitchen tonight, and start off tomorrow morning at breakfast."

Old Robert nodded, but sighed inwardly. He remembered the breakfasts her father had preferred ... half a grapefruit, orange juice, tiny rolls. ...

He need not have worried. It was a glorious morning, and a silver dew lay on leaf and lawn, turning every spider web in the solid macrocarpa hedge into gossamer. Roberta had wakened to hear a *tui* singing in the kowhai tree that bloomed as golden as any English laburnum near her window.

Today Roberta O'More didn't care a rap for Muir Buchanan and his glowering looks of the night before. ... She was back here at Heatherleigh, on a spring morning in Maoriland. She sang as she tripped gaily downstairs to the kitchen.

She served breakfast in the little morning-room that opened off the kitchen. It was dusty and obviously unused,

13

but she flicked a duster over the table in the rounded window, and darted out to pick a vaseful of daffodils.

Ishbel Mackenzie, the honey-haired bride Robert had brought to Heatherleigh from Midlothian sixty years ago, had loved this room.

Roberta served her grandfather with a generous helping of the oatmeal porridge she had soaked the night before. Robert looked cheered. He handed the sugar bowl across to her.

"Mebbe you like your oatmeal sweet?"

She shook her head and reached out for the salt. Under a covered dish Robert found bacon and eggs piping hot, and there was a pile of buttery toast, great substantial slices, not even cut into fingers, he noted gratefully, and the coffee was all that coffee should be.

It was just as well Roberta had not expected a paean of praise for this effort – knowing her grandfather of old, she was more than content with his "No' so bad," as he replaced his napkin in its silver ring.

After breakfast, Robert, according to immemorial custom, went to his study to deal with estate matters, and Roberta, having duly inspected the contents of the refrigerator and found it surprisingly well stocked, went upstairs to make the beds, while Donald coped with the dishes.

She had dusted her bedroom and Grandy's, and decided the other rooms must wait another day as she was on her mettle today to produce a good lunch. She wasn't at all sure about the stove, as though it was electric it was unlike any Roberta had ever used, being a heat storage type, that stayed hot all day.

Halfway down the last flight of stairs was a picture of Ishbel Mackenzie, her honey-gold hair piled high in the Edwardian curls of her day, a full tartan skirt clipped about the trim waist with wide leather belt, and a heavy ivory silk blouse, all embroidery and tucks, fitting up against her slim throat. Her eyes were that shade between green and brown, the same colour as Roberta's eyes, but Ishbel had a height Roberta lacked.

The door from the study opened, and Robert Heatherleigh came quietly up the stairs to where Roberta stood gazing at his dead wife's portrait.

The old man looked at her a moment, searchingly, from under his shaggy brows, and said gruffly: "Why did you suddenly decide to come to Heatherleigh, Roberta?"

She turned from her contemplation of the portrait and gazed into the stern face above hers. She looked down into the great hall at the bottom of the stairs, through the open doorway to the terrace beyond, to the pictures on the walls, paintings of long-dead Heatherleighs and Mackenzies, and back to her grandfather's face again.

"My roots are here," she said simply, and would have said more . . . would have told him of the heart-hunger she had always known for Heatherleigh, of all that it had stood for in the gay, artificial life she had known in the bohemian circles her parents had loved: but at that moment, over her grandfather's shoulder, she caught a movement in the hall below.

Muir Buchanan was leaning against the study doorpost, his fierce dark eyes fixed on her in a look that disconcerted her. Could anything Muir had put into her grandfather's mind have prompted his question just now?

"I'm going to pick some flowers now," she said lightly, and moved down, nodded carelessly to Muir, and picked up a pair of scissors. Ten minutes later she heard Muir's horse being ridden away.

The next morning, her first conscious thought was that today George would be home. As she ran across the lawn Roberta noticed that the buds of the lilac were dark and swelling, and the laburnums were showing yellow at the tips of their swinging tassels . . . a day fit to welcome George back into her life again.

He had been fourteen when last she had seen him; that made him twenty-seven now. Muir had called him a braw laddie then, Young George had been a hero to the small Roberta. He had known all sorts of things, about which she had been ignorant . . . country lore, and bird-watching: he had been fearless and brave, and very ready

15

to share Roberta's portion of the blame for the scrapes they had so frequently been involved in – had Roberta but allowed it.

Don't let George be changed, God, she asked in her heart.

The phone rang. It was the garage in Oamaru to say that Roberta's car was ready. She decided to go in for it right away, then she would probably be home before George arrived. She was dismayed to find there was no afternoon bus.

Grandfather chuckled.

"We consider ourselves lucky at Heatherleigh to have one bus a day. It goes in during the morning and comes back in the afternoon. But it's all right. Muir's leaving with a load of sheep in the waggon at one o'clock for Waiareka Saleyards. It's a very short distance from there into town. You can go in with him."

It was a pleasant drive through the North Otago countryside, gentle and rolling . . . every so often they caught glimpses of the blue Pacific, and distant headlands encircling the bays on the east coast. Over to the west the Kakanui Ranges continued the line of the Alps, and were still slightly crowned with snow.

Their way led over innumerable bridges crossing the Wainakarua and Kakanui Rivers with the sweet water flowing beneath and the willows clustering close. There was only one thing to spoil the drive. . . .

"Sorry there's a following wind, Roberta," said Muir, wrinkling his nostrils and grinning. The smell of sheep from the two-tier waggon behind the cab of the truck was rather strong.

"But I don't really mind it . . . much," said Roberta, sniffing. "Strange, we were outside Paris once. We'd gone there for an exhibition and Daddy was in the forest, painting. Mother was reading and I wandered away on the outskirts till I came to a farm. It was so tiny . . . the field so green and lush, and ruled-off looking, not like our great barbed-wire-fenced paddocks here. There were just a half a dozen ewes and their lambs in it, Muir. I leaned over the little stone

16

wall, and from the ground there came up to me the unmistakable smell of sheep."

Roberta closed her eyes briefly, re-living that remembrance. "And I felt deadly homesick for Heatherleigh."

Muir looked at her quickly from under his overhanging brows.

"Had Heatherleigh meant so much to you, Roberta? I mean – it was just one month out of your life." His tone was derisive.

Roberta remained silent. She could have told the Muir of years ago just what Heatherleigh had meant to her . . . but not this dark-visaged, antagonistic man.

"Yes," was all she said.

By this time they had turned off the main road and were driving along Thousand-acre Road that loped over hill and dale, from the sea, to the coalmine, an open-cast one, at Airedale. They swung around by the village of Weston at the Old Manse corner, and along to Waiareka.

They pulled up at the stockyards. Muir got down and said:

"Don't be in a hurry to walk on yet, Roberta," and went across to where a big Chevrolet had just pulled in, and from which an elderly man was emerging.

He came back. "That's a farmer I know. His niece is dropping him here and driving into town. She'll give you a lift."

The car wasn't quite ready, after all, so Roberta filled in the time window-shopping. When the repairs had been completed, they had tried the car out and noticed a whine in the engine, something to do with the water-pump probably.

Oamaru was as attractive as she had remembered . . . wide, tree-lined streets, with cars parked on the angle between the double row of trees in the middle, white stone buildings, the older ones greying, not quite so many corrugated iron roofs as in most New Zealand cities, but more orange-tiled ones.

She decided to have a cup of tea, and immediately caught sight of the National Club's sign. Of course . . . Grandy

17

would consider it almost treasonable to go anywhere else, she supposed. Naturally, he was a dyed-in-the-wool Tory. Roberta hadn't sorted out her impressions of New Zealand politics yet, though she had an idea that in this progressive country there wasn't a great gulf between the two parties anyway ... still, it would be nice to settle down and develop rigid ideas on the subject one way or another.

Roberta went across to a secluded table in a corner and sat down. The waitresses were busy, and as she waited her thoughts inevitably drifted to George. He was a distant cousin, extremely distant, on old Robert Heatherleigh's grandfather's side, so George was a Heatherleigh.

His folk had migrated to West Australia, and Roberta's mother had looked them up once when they were visiting Perth. Then, when Daddy had gone to Borneo for a month's painting, and wanted Mother with him, Mrs. O'More had taken Roberta and George across to New Zealand for that never-to-be-forgotten month. Perhaps George would carry on the estate for Heatherleigh. It would be so fitting. George had loved the land, and had vowed he would go farming when he grew up, though of course he might have changed his mind half a dozen times since.

A shadow fell across her. She looked up. It was Muir, cutting across her pleasant dreams of George. Roberta came back to reality immediately.

"I thought you'd probably make for here," Muir said. "I finished early at the yards."

Roberta's voice was cool.

"Oh, you needn't have bothered. I'm not a bit lonely. I've junketed about the world on my own too much for that."

Muir said, a hint of amusement in his tone, "I wasn't looking for you. I haven't got much patience with people who are lonely on their own – I'm to meet someone here. It just occurred to me as I came up the stairs that you might have found your way up here."

Roberta's ready colour rose. He had a knack of putting her in the wrong.

A tall, dark man came in, looked around, and made for

18

their table. Muir introduced them, and added, for Roberta's benefit,

"The Member of Parliament for North Otago."

The Member was charmed to meet Robert Heatherleigh's granddaughter, and said so. Roberta suggested easily that she should leave the men to their discussion, but Muir shook his head and ordered tea for three.

"We'll go into the office after this, and get the business done there."

Roberta decided she would finish her tea quickly and leave early just the same.

Nevertheless, as she headed up the South Hill with its glorious blaze of rock plants overhanging its terraces, she noticed Muir was on her heels, in the truck. As she left the main road and hit the shingle one, she thought without shame that it served him right if he collected her dust all the way home.

He didn't take the turn-off to Buchanan, but followed her right into the courtyard where the cars were garaged, pulled up his truck, and was waiting to open the car door for her when she turned off the ignition.

They came into the great hall together. Grandy was standing on the hearthrug, Skipper, the brindled bull terrier, beside him.

A sound from above attracted Roberta's attention. She looked up . . . George!

Had she met him in a crowd there would still have been instant recognition. This was exactly as she would have expected George to look at twenty-seven . . . tall, broad-shouldered, thick, straight hair sweeping back from a broad brow, a strong nose, firm chin. He had a beautiful parting – George, who in that long-ago time used to have a funny all-over cut at the barber's to save the bother of finding his parting.

There was a sudden, startled moment of recognition, then they both moved, Roberta running lightly up the stairs as if her feet were winged, her golden hair bobbing at every step, a small girl in a light-weight green woollen suit, open at the throat, a string of milky pearls against the pale brown of her skin.

They met with outstretched hands and each other's name spoke in unison. This indeed was a welcome home. Without hesitation Roberta lifted her cheek to George. Equally unhesitating, he turned her chin around and kissed her on the lips.

Roberta wheeled about, laughing, and looked straight down at Muir, standing where she had left him, feet apart, arms folded, an unreadable expression on his face. She felt resentment flare within her. He probably thinks that at least someone is glad to see me home, she thought.

Muir turned away, gave Robert Heatherleigh some notes of advice about the sale of the sheep, and was gone with a curt word of goodbye to them, flung over his shoulder.

Silence settled on them all. Roberta walked out on to the porch and watched Muir's tall figure turn in the direction of the courtyard. George had followed her out.

She said forlornly, all gladness gone, "I thought Muir would have been glad to have us back here."

"You'll soon find out why he isn't," said George.

George's words concerning Muir Buchanan stayed with Roberta all through dinner, making her uneasy. Perhaps she had been foolish to dream of finding Heatherleigh, and the people she had loved so much, the same as of old.

George seemed restless too. They had talked themselves out after dinner with do-you-remembers, and odd snippets of news out of both their lives to fill up the years in between. Later they sat around the fire in the green hall, pulling the screens around, but somehow there was no feeling of intimacy.

Roberta did some darning. She had an overflowing darning basket beside her and was endeavouring to catch up on the mountainous pile of socks she had collected. Grandy had been amused at her indignation over them. He and Donald had just bought new ones as the holes appeared, he told her. Then he chuckled and said:

"You've a real Scots streak in you after all, despite your upbringing."

Roberta had sighed. Grandy too probably thought they had lived wildly and extravagantly. But all she said aloud was:

"The French are thrifty. I learned to market well, and to sew and embroider."

George still fidgeted. Grandy looked up once impatiently from his book as George turned from station to station on the radio.

"Your stay in the city unsettled you, George?"

George shrugged and laughed, lit another cigarette, and finally decided he would go to bed and read. Grandy yawned and said he wouldn't be long either.

Roberta made them some supper, pushed the undarned socks back in the basket and went upstairs herself. She stood looking out of the window. The garden lay drenched in liquid moonlight: the orchard boughs were a mass of shimmering radiance under the whiteness of it; from below her window came the heady fragrance of narcissi and violets: under the trees, through the lush grass, myriads of daffodils gleamed palely . . . fancy going to bed early on a night like this! Quietly she slipped downstairs, and out by a side door.

Till now she had not had time to explore the old garden. Her steps took her across the side garden to a low stone wall that skirted the orchard and dropped down the slope to the great walnut grove. A cedar spread its aromatic branches over the wall, and beyond its shadows, the moonlight spilled in a pool of bleached white.

Roberta stooped and picked a spray of velvety brown wallflowers that grew in a cranny of the wall. She put up a hand, took hold of a cedar branch and swung herself on to the wall.

It was a still night, magic and spellbinding. Somewhere a sleepy bird stirred, twittered, and slept again. There was a movement from under the walnuts and every now and then a queer snuffling. Hedgehogs, of course. She relaxed.

Suddenly she heard a noise that was different from the

natural flutterings and stirrings of the night creatures going about their lawful occasions, a step on the outside lawn, coming nearer, coming purposefully, towards the wall where she was perched.

Roberta smiled dreamily, keeping still. It would be George; he must have heard her come downstairs.

The tall figure moved into the pool of radiance ... Muir, smoking the inevitable pipe.

"I saw you come from the house, Roberta. I'd come back to see if I could have a word with you, but I saw all the lights were out. I was just going back over the stile when I heard the door open and close."

He came close to her as she sat on the wall, the knees of his stained breeches brushing against the soft folds of her full skirt. Roberta had to put her head back to look up at him.

She spoke rather breathlessly – why, she couldn't imagine.

"You've not left Henk sleeping alone, have you, Muir?"

He shook his head, and smiled, his teeth showing white in his dark face.

"No, I should never leave a sleeping child alone in a house at night, Roberta. His aunt is there. She brought over a pile of Henk's socks she'd washed and mended, and an apple pie for our dinner tomorrow, and she's knitting by the fire."

"It was good of you to take Henk, Muir. It can't be easy."

"No. But he's a grand little companion ... the benefits aren't all on his side. I've no son, and at times it was lonely. Henk needs security. He's known sudden bereavement, and an uprooting." He smiled again. "Henk and I have such good times together."

Roberta suddenly remembered the good times she had known with Muir, thirteen years ago. Muir didn't seem a forbidding, enigmatic stranger any more. There was no antagonism between them, for the moment, in this moonlit garden.

"I still think Henk is a very lucky boy, Muir. You took such care of us, all those years ago, and you must have been very young yourself."

22

He laughed, his dark eyes glinting down on her.

"I've an idea that then you regarded me as almost in the sere and yellow leaf, though . . . didn't you?"

Roberta's one dimple, that gave her face a comical, lopsided look, appeared.

"Well . . . wouldn't you regard anyone like that, who was old enough to spank you?"

"Did I spank you hard?"

"Did you not? I still tingle at the remembrance. I'll wager George does too."

They both laughed, reminiscently, then Muir said: "You've not been across to Buchanan yet?"

"I haven't been asked," she said.

He took the pipe from between his teeth and said:

"The Roberta of a dozen years ago wouldn't have needed an invitation. You had the run of my rooms over the stables, then, didn't you?"

"You're not quite the same Muir, you see," she said.

He accepted that.

"Well . . . will you come? Tomorrow morning? About ten? Have morning tea with me?"

She said, impulsively: "Don't go to any fuss, will you?"

He raised his eyebrows at her.

"I mean I shan't expect it to be kept as if there was a woman about the place."

He looked at her oddly. Oh dear, was she getting offsides with Muir again? Had she sounded condescending?

Muir looked down at the hand on her knee that still held the spray of wallflowers. He lifted it, hand and all, to his nose, sniffing appreciatively.

"Wallflowers are favourites of mine," he said. "They grow thickly around Buchanan. My mother loved them."

Roberta suddenly remembered something her grandfather had told her . . . that Muir had come out to the Dominion because he couldn't settle in his Scots home after his mother died. She couldn't remember Muir ever speaking of his mother before.

The small hand in Muir's large one trembled.

"What are you shaking for?" he asked lazily. He sounded amused. Surely to goodness he didn't think she was trembling because he was so near . . . and there was a moon . . . heavens! A fine scorn possessed her. What did he think she was? – An inexperienced miss out of the schoolroom?

She thought of the gay company she had known in the artistic world her parents had lived in and loved . . . the light banter and the ready wit, the idle flirtations that didn't mean a thing.

Before she could speak Muir said softly:

"Are you cold, Roberta? You should have had a wrap on, perhaps." He looked down at her. She was wearing a soft, fine woollen dress in beechy brown.

He took her other hand, slipped his warm hands up to her cool wrists, then to her elbows where they stayed, his thumbs resting in the soft hollows on the inside of her elbows. She had a moment of panic. Muir was going to kiss her. . . . She leaned back from him a little.

He said: "Things have certainly changed between us, haven't they, Roberta?"

She moistened her suddenly dry lips with her tongue.

"What do you mean, Muir?"

She thought she knew . . . once she was the cherished granddaughter on his employer's estate, he a shepherd lad, not long out from Scotland, told to see she didn't get into any mischief or danger . . . and now. . . .

"I mean," he said, "that the years lessen as we grow older – that where once we were man and child, now we are man and woman."

He took his hands from her arms, put them about her trim waist, and lifted her down.

"Just remember that, will you?" He didn't kiss her. He turned her around to face the house, walked with her in silence to the door at the side, opened it, said goodnight, and went away.

As Roberta tumbled sleepily into bed, she thought, why, Muir didn't say what he wanted to see me about. At the time she had thought it would be about her grandfather. She supposed Muir had got sidetracked ... perhaps the moonlight stirred even the veins of a dour Scot!

She smiled mischievously to herself in the darkness, for it certainly wasn't like Muir to get sidetracked. She sat up in bed suddenly. Perhaps he had said what he wanted to ... but why come all the way from Buchanan to ask her to come to tea? Suddenly she realised Muir wasn't pleased that George had come back. In the moonlight, Muir had seemed more like his old self, whimsical, understanding. ... Moonlight did that, of course ... softened the outlines. Better watch yourself, Roberta, she thought. There are undercurrents beneath the pleasant surface of the Heatherleigh life.

CHAPTER TWO

As Roberta walked over the narrow bridge that spanned the Waianakarua she thought it was a pity that Grandy had sold that part of the estate . . . it was so beautiful. The river cut deeply into the cliff here, and curved around the thickly wooded hillside.

She heard the clippety-clop of horses' hooves coming around the bend in the road, more than one rider by the sound of it. She caught a brief glimpse of chestnut flanks as they swung off the road through the bush, to the track that led to the ford.

She paused, one hand on the railing. She loved to watch horses crossing a ford, picking their way carefully. She put up a hand to shade her eyes as they came into the open.

It was Muir, mounted on his own hack, and leading a mare. Roberta called out softly but clearly, so as not to startle the horses, and he stopped just at the water's edge.

He smiled up at her.

"Oh, you're early. I thought I'd bring you a mount to save you the walk . . . you still ride, I suppose?"

Roberta nodded.

"Yes. I used to hire a hack wherever we were, if I could. Wait there, Muir, and I'll scramble down."

She walked to the end of the bridge and swung down through the willows.

"Good thing you're wearing slacks," said Muir, eyeing her green corduroys. He had dismounted and was holding the reins loosely. He let them drop now. The horses put their muzzles into the clear water, blowing delicately first.

Roberta put her foot into his hand as she had been wont to do as a child, and was up. They took the stony incline gently, and came out on to the metalled road. Dragonflies darted about in the narrow cutting, New Zealand fuchsias, the sweet *koninis* as the Maoris called them, leaned out from the

26

banks with pale apricot bark, and *koromikos*, the native veronicas, gleamed ruby and purple in the dim greenness.

There were wild daisies, and here and there clumps of red clover and lucerne and St. John's wort. The air was close and aromatic. In a lovely *totara* tree near by, a bellbird chimed. Roberta and Muir reined in the horses to catch a glimpse of the friendly green bird. Then they came out of the dark cutting into strong sunlight, rounded the hill, and there before them lay Buchanan.

Roberta reined in the mare again, and remained perfectly still in the saddle from sheer surprise. She had expected a square, four-roomed bungalow, neat, because Muir was a tidy man, with trim painted outhouses, and perhaps a tin-roofed garage stuck conveniently close to the hedge.

Buchanan was set back against the smooth green hill where once, long ago, she and George had rolled from top to bottom for the sheer sensation. It was wide-set and roofed with orange tiles. Its eaves slanted low over rough-cast and brick walls, and there was a wide terrace with a rock edge that was thickly draped with aubrietia just coming into bloom. The rock garden below was a blaze of sun-plants, and beneath the terrace was a huge oval bed of anemones and ranunculi.

The drive, of white, smooth Oamaru shingle, curved around between herbaceous borders that would be rich with bloom and scent in summertime, and over to the left, beyond a hawthorn hedge that would be rose and ivory in November, daffodils ran riot through the orchard.

All about the house, on three sides, clustered the trees, English poplars and oaks, dark pines and cypresses, birches and sycamores, and running up the hill beyond, a delightful plantation of native trees, *taupatas*, *kowhais*, *totaras*, *manuka*, and here and there Australian gums and ribbon-woods.

"The trees in the garden itself are not very tall yet," said Muir. "Yes, I planted a lot, but the ones further back, the tallest, were here when I came. Do you remember this was where the old burnt-out cottage stood? Just two chimneys

27

left standing. I was fortunate, I just had to fell two trees to build."

They cantered up the drive, turned their horses into a white-railed enclosure near the house and went in through the back door.

The sunlight fell through the open door on to the rather bare black-and-white-floored kitchen. There was a white, scrubbed table (he must get a woman in to achieve that, thought Roberta), an electric stove, an open fireplace, with a brass rail across it, a stainless steel sink and bench, plain yellow cotton curtains at the windows, and a mantel littered with pipes, and bits of harness, letters and rubbish. There were a couple of good leather chairs and a large rag rug.

Through an open doorway she saw a very small room evidently built for sole use as an office with a built-in desk, various notes and lists pinned up on the walls, and a filing cabinet.

"I'll show you through first," said Muir.

There were two empty bedrooms, small ones, and Muir's. It was quite what one would expect of a man's room, furnished by a man ... plain furniture, solid and comfortable; drapes with a tailored effect, curtains well pushed back from the sunny windows, a good carpet underfoot.

The books gave character to the room. There were rather more shelves than usual in a bedroom, and they were filled with shabby, much-read books, with here and there a bright new jacket that indicated a mind that wasn't static, but read widely.

On the bedside table were half a dozen books ... a couple of whodunits from the library in Oamaru, a textbook on soil conservation, a theological study book, a Bible, and a huge copy of Robert Burns.

Roberta chuckled: "I believe you read this as often as you read your Bible," she said.

"Burns could aye say it well," he said, and showed her into Henk's room.

It was an odd, fascinating shape, with an alcove end. There was a tartan rug on the bed, the sort of rug a boy could sprawl on, reading, and not be worrying if his shoes were dirty. The bookshelves were filled with books and boys' magazines, and in the alcove was a large deal table with a Hornby train set with signals and tunnels and a half-built station of miniature bricks on it.

A sturdy seat ran under the corner window. Roberta had a sudden vision of the happy hours a boy could spend there, looking out, thinking the long, long thoughts of youth. There was a glass case with birds' eggs and nests in it, neatly labelled, that recalled Muir's instructions to George of years ago, never to take more than one egg, and to take only last year's nests.

On the walls were pictures of Henk's parents, and some of the Dutch royal family, and for the rest, prints of trains, aeroplanes and ships pinned up.

The drawing-room was comfortable, with deep chairs, more books, a good piano. It had french windows opening out on to a porch that looked as if it was used a lot: there were cane chairs and tables, copies of *Punch*, the *Scotsman*, the *Auckland Weekly*, digests and comics.

Coming out of there, she indicated a door opposite.

Muir hesitated, then said: "Another empty room," and passed on.

He took her back to the kitchen for morning tea. She sat on the table and swung her legs while he buttered fresh girdle-scones and oatcakes. Roberta cocked an eye at them as he set them on the yellow checked cloth.

"Make your own, Muir?"

He nodded.

"My speciality for visitors."

He lifted the kettle and began pouring the water into the brown teapot.

Roberta's voice sounded rueful.

"It's humiliating to any woman to see a man so deft . . . so self-sufficient. You wouldn't have any need of a wife, would you, Muir Buchanan?"

He looked at her with something grim in his expression. He swung her off the table, put a hand to her shoulder, and marched her through the hall to the room at the front he had not showed her. He opened the door and propelled her in.

This was evidently meant for the best bedroom. There was a fireplace, and french windows on to a small porch that in turn looked out on the rose garden. The pillars were wreathed in wistaria.

The room was quite bare except for built-in bookcases under the windows, and two wardrobes flush with the walls. Muir opened another door that led off it. A small apartment, but sunny. There were built-in linen presses, with tiny drawers and shelves. Obviously a nursery.

Roberta took it all in, turned to Muir. He was waiting, watching her, arms folded.

He said: "A man doesn't want a wife just to bake girdle-scones and oatcakes, and sweep his floors, Roberta."

She flushed, and was about to speak when they heard the phone ring.

"Excuse me," said Muir, and left her.

She didn't know quite what to do. Most people liked telephone conversations to be private, so she stayed where she was. She drew her own conclusion. Muir had built this for someone . . . and something had happened. She must have rubbed salt in the wounds by accusing him of self-sufficiency. She went to the window, came back, and aimlessly, to fill in time, opened the top drawer of one of the presses. She expected it to be empty. It wasn't.

Marie's photograph stared up at her. Here in a room around which Muir had built a dream. It was in a gilt frame, but the glass was broken. But even through the splintered fragments she could see that the early promise of beauty that the young Marie had shown had flowered to full maturity.

Strange, she would have thought Muir Buchanan would have had more discrimination than to lose his heart to anyone as soulless and calculating as Marie Sylvester. No wonder Muir was cynical and distrusting. . . . As a lad he would have been vulnerable and idealistic in his loving. Roberta hastily but silently closed the drawer.

She was coming out of the bedroom into the hall when he returned.

She said, softly, "Sorry, Muir, that was a stupid remark of mine." Then, to ease the tension, "And it satisfies my ego to know you *aren't* self-sufficient."

She might just as well not have made the gesture of apology. Muir said nothing, merely returned her to the kitchen. Odd, and infuriating that her grandfather's one-time shepherd could make her feel that she had committed a social blunder. She had a sense of having pried, too. Roberta poured the tea, her hand unsteady, yet glad of something to do. It wasn't often that small talk deserted Roberta.

They drank their tea in silence. Muir reached for his pipe and lit it.

"Muir," said Roberta, "you're the one to tell me, I think – is Grandy as wealthy as he used to be?"

Muir sat quite still for a moment, without answering, then he said:

"Yes. I can reassure you on that. More wealthy probably. Wool prices have been good, of course. You have no need to worry. His bank balance and his investments are very healthy. Of course he spends a lot on the community, but there'll be plenty left." His tone was derisive again.

"That's good," returned Roberta cheerfully, determined to ignore this man's moods. "It was just that Heatherleigh seemed so shabby – I know these big places are hard to maintain, so I wondered how things were financially."

"It's not that . . . it's just not being able to get help in the house. They did try with one or two young girls from the village as maids. but with no woman to oversee their work, they slacked and were more trouble than they were worth. It's not lack of money."

"That's a load off my mind," said Roberta.

Muir seemed to be having trouble with his pipe, and couldn't get it to draw properly. He rose impatiently, and went over to the fireplace, knocking it out.

"I can quite believe it would be," said Muir.

Roberta wondered if she only imagined there was a shade of contempt in his voice. She said hastily:

"Muir, may I use your phone for a toll call? I'd like to ring Auckland, and I'd rather not put this call through at home."

Muir put his pipe back in the pipe rack.

"Oh, yes, go ahead. The phone is in the hall. It may take some time to get through, of course. I'm going to settle to some work in the office. You could read while you're waiting."

"Oh, I'm going to make it an urgent call. I'm more likely to get my friend now than at any other time."

She got through surprisingly quickly.

"Is that you, Meg? Yes, it really is. . . . I'm ringing from Heatherleigh village, not from the big house, though. I didn't want to ring from there in case you can't do this, and it would disappoint my grandfather if he knew there was the chance of it.

"Now, Meg, if you decide not to, it will be all right, it's not anything that can be decided in a hurry. Only I hope you can, because it would be so ideal, and the children would love it. So would you."

A long pause, then a chuckle from Roberta. "Yes, all right, I'll stop being maddening and come to the point . . . well, here I come. Heatherleigh is as beautiful as I remembered it, only more so. Grandfather is a pet, but he and old Donald have no permanent help in the house. There's loads of room, Meg, and I wondered if you would care to take on the position of housekeeper? I've found out that the school is excellent and a bus calls each morning for the high school children and takes them into Waitaki High School . . . didn't you once tell me John was educated at Waitaki? I mean David would be ready for High in another year, and as for Josephine, she'd be in her element in the stables here.

"There's a wing of the house that used to be for the exclusive use of the servants . . . it's delightful, Meg. We could have it done up, and it would be much more of a home for the children than ever the flat has been. I know how worried you've been, out all day, and the children home

32

before you. David wouldn't get into mischief here, there's so much for him to do . . . the things he loves, too. I realised this could be the answer to all your problems, and would help solve mine too. Grandy is in a position to pay well. I've just made sure of that.

"Yes, I'm staying on. Grandy needs someone of his own. I've rung Supplefits and they think I can carry on my work down here, as I don't want to give it up. Now I'm going to see if I can rig up the rooms over the stable as a studio. And listen, Meg, I know you couldn't decide without seeing the place. There are still a few days of the school holidays left. What about parking the children at your aunt's for a few days, and coming down by plane? Take the plane to Taeri Aerodrome near Dunedin, and I'll meet you there. No trouble, it's only about eighty miles. Well . . . think it over and ring me tonight. I'll give you the number, it's the Oamaru exchange. You can ask me anything else you think of tonight. I may be very guarded, of course, if Grandy is about. Bye-bye, Meg, my love to the imps."

Roberta's eyes were sparkling as she danced into the kitchen. Muir got up from his desk. Roberta gave a little skip of pure delight as a child might have done as she came through the doorway. Even Muir's enmity and disapproval couldn't shadow the joy of the moment.

"You heard? That's a friend of mine, who had the flat next door. She's a widow, and has a boy of eleven, and a girl of eight. She went back to teaching, domestic science, cooking branch. Her husband was a farmer, and she hates the city now. I hope she takes a fancy to Heatherleigh. If she doesn't, I'll just have to make looking after the house a full-time job for myself."

"Would you do even that, Roberta?"

She wrinkled her brow. What was he getting at now? It was beyond her. She ignored it, and plunged on, too delighted at the chance of being able to do something for Heatherleigh to delve deeper.

"Yes, of course. What else could I do? Only it's too much

for one woman. I'd like to see Heatherleigh kept as it used to be. If Meg came I could leave the cooking to her, and she and Donald could manage the downstairs section between them. If we got a girl I could probably manage the bedrooms and still keep up with my studio work."

"You don't want to give it up? It means too much to you?"

"Yes, it means a lot. I've worked hard for this particular job, it pays well, and I can keep it going from here."

"Particular job . . . then you don't just paint, and exhibit, and sell?"

Roberta shook her head.

"Oh, it's not like that at all, Muir. It's commercial art. I do the illustrations for corset adverts. I love it."

Muir gazed at her.

"Corsets!" he said, and burst out laughing.

Roberta joined in. "Yes, I know it's funny when you think how soulful Daddy was about subjects, but my work thrills me as much as his did him, and it pays a darned sight better. Where Daddy saw landscapes as landscapes, I see those lines translated into beauty of form, moulded into Supplefit's foundations."

"You leave me lost in wonder," he said. "Have you been doing this for long?"

"Yes, but not in such a big way at first, of course. I've kept myself with that ever since I left school. Someone just had to have a steady income with Daddy so erratic and moving on to fresh scenes every time he got a decent sale. A cheque to Daddy was just a passport to new scenes."

Roberta looked at the kitchen clock.

"Goodness, I'll have to be going, but first I must ring the exchange and find out what that phone call was."

Muir put out a hand to stop her.

"Let me stand the cost of it . . . the bill won't be in for weeks anyway."

She was firm about it, rang them, came back and paid him.

Muir said: "Take the chestnut mare, Roberta. I was going to ask you if you would exercise her for me. Heatherleigh stables have gone to the pack, and George is riding the only spare hack. So you can have Clancy.''

Her delight was swift and transforming. "I'll take care of her, Muir.''

"I know you will. Now off with you. Farmers must work!''

He came out with her, whistled to the mare. He had carrots for Clancy and for his own mare, Sally. Roberta took one from him, loving the feel of the velvet muzzle against her palm. Muir put out his hand for Roberta's sandalled foot, and swung her into the saddle. She turned back just before she reached the cutting to wave, but Muir hadn't waited to watch her, and was striding towards his car, whistling, *"Gan on the forty-second, gan on the forty-twa."*

Inexplicable, this man, sternly antagonistic one moment, making the friendly gesture of lending her a mount the next. But what odds? What was Muir Buchanan to her?

Roberta found it was after twelve by the time she reached Heatherleigh. She would have to hustle to have lunch ready by one. Something quick and light, an omelette, perhaps . . . she could get the men rounded up before she actually served it – omelettes didn't brook delay.

George came into the kitchen, tall, handsome, but scowling.

"Oh, there you are, Roberta. Where on earth have you been?''

"Over at Buchanan . . . but Grandfather knew. Didn't you ask?''

George scowled more than ever.

"I did ask the old man and he merely grunted and said: 'Oh, she's awa' out somewhere on the estate. Roberta was aye fond of a prowl on her own.' I wanted you to ride with me. I thought you could have taken his nag.''

Roberta chuckled.

"Maybe Grandy's memory isn't all it used to be, and he'd not like to admit it. He probably forgot where I'd said I was

35

going. Never mind. Muir's offered me his chestnut mare to exercise."

"Well, would you ride with me this afternoon?"

She shook her head ruefully. She would love to have gone. George's friendliness and his eagerness for her company acted like balm on her spirit after a morning like this had been.

"Sorry, George. I'd simply love it, but I must get on with the cleaning, as I gallivanted off this morning. I've got a friend coming down from Auckland for a day or two, and I'd like to have the place fairly decent for her.

"I'm going to clear out the servants' quarters this afternoon. They're appalling after being shut up so long. Then some time soon I'll turn Muir's old quarters over the stable into a studio for myself."

George looked at her and smiled, a very nice smile.

"Then you are going to stay? Good."

Roberta told her grandfather after dinner, when he had retired to the study with a pipe, that she was going to stay on and continue her work as an illustrator of advertisements.

"It will mean frequent trips to Auckland by plane, every two or three months, but if you'll have me, I'll stay."

Old Robert looked at her with eyes that had grown a little misty.

"If I'll have you," he repeated. "Oh, lassie!" and he pulled her down on the chair beside him.

"You'll not need to work, Roberta, I've more than plenty."

She said simply: "I've *got* to work, Grandy, I can't help it."

Robert nodded. She was a chip off the old block . . . he too had found fierce joy in work. The ability to work stood you in good stead when you needed it.

He could hear Ishbel's voice saying: "I'm so grateful there's so much to do, Rob," in the dark days after Dugald's horse had returned home riderless one evening and they had found him on the tussocks under Windy Crag, still and cold, his face turned upwards to the sky.

He had been glad of the demanding, thought-banishing work of mustering, dipping, shearing, and harvesting thirty years ago, when he knew that when he returned to the house Ishbel would no longer be there to greet him. His gladness that there was work to occupy the hours had repeated itself over and over ... when young Robert had died so suddenly and unexpectedly of meningitis, and when Ian had been killed so foolishly and so tragically.

Robert hoped Roberta would never need the anodyne of work as he had needed it, but you could never tell, and the need and will to work was one of life's greatest blessings.

While he was thinking of all this, Roberta added: "Besides, I like to pay my way."

Old Robert turned his head against the back of the chair so that she should not see the tear that was rolling down his weatherbeaten cheek, and said gruffly: "I don't doubt I've been a bit hard in my time, lass, but I'm inclined to think I've mellowed, and I should think we'd do well wi' each other ... but I know full well it'll be harder for you doing your illustrating down here – and you're doing it for me, and I appreciate it. There's just one thing I'm set on. I'll pay your fares up to Auckland, and ... don't deny me the pleasure of buying you things now and then, will you?"

Roberta knew when it was wise to be independent, and when it was gracious to give in.

"Thank you Grandy." She rose. "And now I must do the dishes, and I want to do some sorting in the servants' wing."

She put her warm young cheek to his for a moment, then rose. At the door she stopped. There was something she wanted to ask, had meant to ever since this morning.

"Tell me, was Muir ever engaged, and was it broken off or something?"

Her grandfather shook his head, positively.

"No ... why?"

"That house of his. He showed me all over it today. He's built a beautiful bedroom at the front, a double bedroom, with a nursery off it. I wondered if he had been jilted, or if someone he loved had died."

What she didn't ask was what she really wanted to know . . what is Marie to him?

Her grandfather had a twinkle in his eye.

"It's not nearly as romantic as that. Muir is a practical man like myself. It's only common sense to plan ahead. Altering a house is nearly as expensive these days as rebuilding. Every man who loves the land thinks in terms of a wife and sons. . . ." he glanced at the disgusted expression on his granddaughter's face, and added with another twinkle, "perhaps even a daughter or two. I daresay, in time, Muir will marry."

Roberta gazed levelly at her grandfather.

"Tell me," she said coolly, "when you asked my grandmother to marry you and come out here, were you thinking in terms of a woman to bear you sons to inherit the land?"

"*Touché!*" cried old Robert, laughing, then, thinking of Muir, still a bachelor, and above thirty, he added: "Not, of course, that Muir is by any means woman-shy."

Roberta wondered what he meant by that.

She came into the kitchen to find George with the dishes dried and neatly stacked. "I'll come and give you a hand with the clearing out," he said.

It reminded Roberta of the time she and George had cleared out the old barn for a playhouse, and was great fun, as it had been then. They got almost as dirty.

Meg rang that night.

"I've got a seat on the morning plane for tomorrow. Is that too soon? If it is, if you can't get away to-morrow, I'll come up from Dunedin by bus. I think I should in any case. It would save you a trip, and there's a bus leaving Dunedin at two-thirty. It could drop me on the Main South Road somewhere . . . Teschemakers or Otepopo, and you could just pick me up there."

Roberta replied firmly that she would meet her at Taeri at one-thirty, and after a short chat went in search of George.

"Would you like me to drive you down, Roberta? It would have to be your car, of course, but—"

Roberta seized on the idea. "I'd love company, and I've never driven over the Kilmog, or Mount Cargill."

Roberta told her grandfather she had a friend coming for a few days. She was prepared to head him off if he was curious, but he simply thought it would be nice for Roberta to have a friend to stay in this male household.

It was a sparkling morning with a hint of late frost in the air, that had brought the gardener out from his cottage soon, to see if his early potatoes, just peeping through, had been blackened.

Roberta was wearing a green corduroy jacket, and her head was bare, and shining in the early sun. George looked at her appreciatively as they rattled over the cattle-stops and headed up the tree-lined lane.

It was a delightful road, winding along the downland of North Otago, the blue hills beyond Palmerston South ahead of them, the river glinting blue between the cuttings as it reflected the sky.

Great soapsuds of clouds piled high over the hills, the willow wands were showing red in the blind basket-maker's cottage on the main road, and the sea came into view every now and then, vividly blue with great white rollers crashing on the golden shore.

The horizon was fascinating, sea and sky seeming to meet so far away. And beyond it all, what? The icy wastes of the South Pole, with who knew what wealth of minerals in its frozen maw.

They stopped at Goodwood to see the seals basking on the rocks below the cliffs.

"Soon they'll be gone," said Roberta. "I wonder if they really go back to Seal Island . . . it makes the world seem so small."

Somewhere between the Kilmog and Mount Cargill, George pulled the car into a bush dell that overlooked a stretch of beach and backwater.

"We'll have lunch here."

It was a delectable spot. *Ngaios* were thickly clustered, myriads of their tiny stars of waxen bloom peeping from under the pointed fans of leaves. The blossom had carpeted the ground. Roberta picked one up, placed it in the palm of her hand, and gazed closely at it.

"The texture of the petals is just like magnolia flowers," she said, "but much daintier."

She spread a rug half in the sun, half in shade, and put a checked cloth on it. George unpacked the hamper with her, their fingers touching now and then. Roberta smiled at him.

"This is so like all we did thirteen years ago. Remember the day we helped Muir burn off all the potato shaws and roasted potatoes in the ashes? They were so hot we had to hold them in paper to eat them. They were black and ashy, and we must have used a terrible lot of butter on them, but nothing since has ever tasted quite so good. Then that time we tried to grill steak on sticks. We wouldn't admit it, but it was half raw, and we did feel squeamish after it."

George said he was just as pleased with the present. They had finished their meal by now, but were too lazy to move.

Roberta laughed up into George's face, so near hers. She was leaning on her right elbow and he on his left, so that their shoulders were touching.

George had been a likeable youngster, and he was certainly a very personable young man. His eyes were bluer than ever, and his chin and well-cut mouth were very firm. There was a hint of something ruthless about George now. It both frightened and excited Roberta.

At times he seemed just the George he used to be, at times a new personality. It would be interesting to explore his mind.

George leaned closer and slipped his arm about her shoulders, drawing her nearer him. Roberta couldn't have moved had she wanted to, for she seemed suddenly powerless. For a moment the vivid colour flamed into her cheeks, as bright as the gipsy scarf she wore knotted loosely about her throat. George kissed her. He released her slightly, looked down at her with a lazy, satisfied smile lifting the corners of his mouth.

All of a sudden Roberta knew embarrassment, hot and shaking, take possession of her. How stupid . . . after all, she had been kissed before! Where was her poise, her confidence? To cover these tumultuous feelings she said quickly, and in mock reproof: "George!"

He laughed and shrugged, sheer mischief dancing in his eyes.

"Why not? Cousins may kiss, you know."

"George!" The reproof sounded genuine this time. "That wasn't a cousinly kiss!"

George put back his head and howled with laughter.

"My darling innocent . . . it wasn't meant to be."

Roberta couldn't help laughing with him. George bent to her again, but Roberta sprang to her feet.

"Come on, we've overstayed as it is, and on these hills anything might happen to delay us."

As they took the long, steady pull up Mount Cargill, with great plantations of blue-gums and vast areas of *manuka*, now in white heathery bloom on either side, George said suddenly:

"It's not a close relationship, is it?"

Roberta looked mischievous.

"It certainly isn't . . . not near enough to give you any privileges . . . we aren't kissing kin. I think it's just that about four generations back our forebears were cousins."

George seemed in no way perturbed that the relationship was so slight.

Soon before them lay the landlocked waters of the harbour within the curve of Otago peninsula, and out beyond lay the open sea. From the comparatively flat area of the wharves and shipping swept the residential suburbs in tier upon tier of multi-coloured roofs, generously interspersed with the green of public gardens and broad swathes of tree-lined avenues.

Grey stone buildings were wreathed in ivy and virginia

creeper, and everywhere on the skyline were graceful spires and bell towers. They swept down to the city.

"George Street, Princes Street," said Roberta, "yet it doesn't need similar street names to make you realise this is the Edinburgh of the south. The whole atmosphere is Scots."

They turned up through the Octagon towards Wakari where they would dip over the hills to Taeri Plain.

Roberta said idly: "You seem to know the road, George."

"I was over it just a month ago. Marie came to the village for a few days. She's not a good sailor and doesn't like the all-night ferry crossing from the North Island, so she flew down. Muir was busy, so he asked me to meet her."

"*Muir* asked you! Why? Didn't she just stay with her uncle and aunt as she did all those years ago?"

George shook his head. "They moved to the Waikato. They prefer cattle and the lush dairy country to a sheeprun. She stayed at the Heatherleigh Arms. Muir has always kept in touch with her."

Yes, of course, thought Roberta. The photograph. Why shouldn't he have done? Marie hadn't left New Zealand as she herself had done, and Marie had been much nearer Muir's age . . . nearly seventeen, a mature seventeen.

She said, as indifferently as she could manage: "Was she down for any particular reason?"

"Just to see Muir, apparently," said George. "She was at Buchanan a lot. They went to Dunedin one night to see the opera, and Muir took a day or two off and ran her around the lakes in the back country . . . Lake Pukaki, with Mount Cook at the head of it, and Lake Tekapo. They say that's a gem, pure turquoise colour . . . Look, straight ahead, there's the airport."

George whistled as Meg stepped off the plane.

"A beauty, isn't she? I imagined something rather prim, you know, well-groomed and sensible, with a matronly bosom . . . domestic science sounds like that. But she's ravishing . . . slim, elegant, redheaded . . . the lass with the delicate air."

42

Roberta was glad he approved. She wanted everyone to like Meg.

Roberta saw at once, from Meg's delight in Heatherleigh, that it would be easy to persuade her to stay. Grandfather had always treated his staff well, and the rooms in the staff wing were wide and sunny and comfortably furnished.

There was still plenty to be done to them, but while Grandy had napped yesterday, Roberta and George had sneaked quite a few items of good furniture down from unused rooms upstairs. There would be more to come, when Grandy knew what was toward.

Meg stood entranced and her eyes roved over it all, taking in all that a home like this could mean to herself and the children. There was a large sitting-room that had served as common-room for the staff. It had a good carpet and a suite in it, a piano that had seen better days, but could be tuned, roomy bookcases and a window-seat that looked out on to a side lawn where a shady elm swept like a tent down to the ground.

Beyond the lawn a slender cherry tree shone in bridal transparency of bloom, and about the windows grew fuchsias whose dry stems were just leafing, and in December would burgeon forth in purple and scarlet.

As well as a large bedroom, there were four small ones, and a bathroom. One of the small rooms opened off the large one, and Roberta had paid special attention to this.

Meg had once said that in the flat one could never get away from the children to live any sort of life of one's own. She had a hobby, though somewhat on the lines of her own job ... writing cookery articles for magazines. Roberta sometimes illustrated them for her.

Roberta and George had brought down a grey and blue Wilton carpet, banished the bed to another room, put in a couple of bookcases, a plain dark table with two serviceable drawers, an easy chair, a standard lamp, and a really charming writing table that had belonged to Robert's mother It was polished rosewood, with delicately curved legs, and drawers that bowed outwards. There was a small embroidery table to match. Roberta had put it into close fellowship with the fireside chair.

By the time Meg had seen the stables, the pools in the river where the children would swim in summer, the delectable kitchen garden, the trees David and Josephine would climb, the litter of puppies in the old barn, the kittens in the grain-shed . . . well, the little room that would be all her own just put the seal on her decision.

"I'll come, Roberta."

Roberta was instantly starry-eyed with delight. Not just because it would mean Heatherleigh would be looked after as it should but because it would mean so much to Meg.

Meg didn't brood, was never bitter, yet under all her brave acceptance of life as it had been since she lost her husband, Roberta had sensed that life in the city stifled her. She had said once, looking at sturdy David and slender, vital Josephine: "John would have hated it for them. . . . He loved the hills and the wide paddocks and the river running down to the sea."

It would be good to have a close friend here. Roberta loved the company of her menfolk, but liked her own sex too, and at times yearned for a cosy gossip over her mending basket.

Meg couldn't go back till the Monday plane. All others were booked out.

"It won't matter, the children don't go back till Tuesday this term, and my classes don't start till Wednesday. My aunt will give the children a wonderful time. It will be at least a month before I can come here permanently, Roberta."

Roberta was glad about that. She intended getting a firm out from Dunedin to spring-clean Heatherleigh. They could shampoo and moth-proof all the carpets, remove the cobwebs from the high ceilings, and dry-clean the upholstered furniture. Roberta hoped to get a couple of girls from the village to help till then, for lambing was in full swing, the men were out early and late, and she seemed to be making tea all day, and the men from the cleaning firm would have to be put up, she supposed.

Grandfather put his foot down over that.

"They can stay at Heatherleigh Arms," he said. Then he twinkled. "We've found out Roberta is an excellent landgirl. We've more use for her outside. I don't want her worn out with housework."

Roberta served a special dinner that night, with help from Meg, to celebrate. She rang Buchanan and invited Muir and Henk over.

"We won't be having it till seven, Muir. Is that a little long for Henk to wait?"

"No, at this time of year we rarely manage it before then, Roberta, so we always have a good afternoon tea at three-thirty when Henk gets in from school, and in the holidays we carry on the same."

Roberta was anxious that Meg should make a good impression on Muir as well as on Grandfather and George. It was quite evident that she did. The crisp auburn hair sprang back from a fine forehead, her tawny eyes gave a hint of character in that they looked at life fairly and squarely. Her voice was delightful too, low and rich in tone, with a hint of amusement in it, and withal she had a certain poise that years of happy marriage had given her.

Now, after dinner, Roberta looked across at her. She was talking to Grandfather, and he was listening intently, his chuckle now and then sounding as Meg's turn of phrase caught his fancy.

Muir had been absorbed in showing Henk a book on English railways that had belonged to Ian Heatherleigh, but as Roberta went across to the window-seat to them, she saw Muir looking across the shadowy room to where Meg and Grandy were. He didn't even notice Roberta till she dropped to the seat beside him.

Roberta said: "Meg's lovely, don't you think? I've used her as a model several times."

"I should think you would," said Muir, and added: "I've aye liked redheads."

There was a silence between them. Roberta was conscious of some emotion she had never before experienced. But how

45

absurd. What could it matter to her if Muir Buchanan liked Titian hair? But ... but she wished she herself had put on something different ... the rich emerald velvet, or the black with the scarlet sash. She needed colour, with her pale locks, and she'd chosen this oatmeal dress!

She turned to find Muir watching her, and hoped her feelings hadn't been mirrored in her face. She wasn't usually as ungenerous in her inward tribute to other women's beauty.

The corners of Muir's mouth lifted a little in amusement.

"But redheads are ill to live with," he said, and spoilt it by adding: "Not that you'd be the easiest, yourself."

Roberta got up and walked away.

Roberta was on her way home from one of her trips to Auckland on business. It was a sparkling day, and the trip down across the North Island had been breathtakingly beautiful, with the lovely coastline spread out like a relief map below them. The only thing that had spoiled the trip was that when she had opened her morning paper, the headlines had carried news of two spectacular air crashes.

She would be glad to get home, but it would be Paraparaumu first, then across the Cook Strait to the South Island. She would have a cup of tea at the cafeteria at Paraparaumu, which was the air centre for Wellington, an hour and a half's bus journey away.

As she came off the tarmac, one man out of the waiting crowd stepped forward and said: "Good morning, Roberta."

Muir!

She blinked. He was the last person she would have expected to see here.

"What on earth are you doing here?"

"Going home on the same plane. In fact, I've got the seat next to you."

"Did you have to come to a Wheat Board sitting?" she asked.

He shook his head. "Not this time. I've just been up for one night." He took her arm. "Come and have a cup of tea."

He was smiling to himself, well pleased. "I've got a surprise for you."

He had. Marie! She was sitting at one of the tables, tea for three in front of her.

Roberta had forgotten how beautiful she was . . . hair that had an even ripple in it like the wind passing over sun-ripened wheat, caught in a Grecian knot at the nape of her neck. Her profile was perfect, her mouth exquisitely curved. She had a skin like magnolia blossom, and her eyes were the blue of the sea. She could have been a figurehead at the prow of some Viking ship.

Her voice was charming, too, with a lilt in it that could do all sorts of things to a man's pulses . . . in fact it was so delightful that you lost sight of the fact that it said very little worth listening to, or had said so little, those years ago.

It was rather hard not to fall under her charm just the same, and all the artist in Roberta responded to her loveliness. They walked out on to the ramp when they had finished their tea.

"Isn't he mad?" said Marie, "coming up all this way for a few hours!"

Muir grinned. "It all depends on how you spend the hours." He added, "I've found them worth while."

Roberta supposed he had.

Marie looked at her watch. "I've got time to see the plane go," she said. It was all just the commonplace, inevitable chatter one usually made on airports and stations and wharves, and none of it meant anything.

Roberta was wearing a new light-weight green suit she had bought in Auckland, with tan accessories, and a very smart bag, but against Marie's black silk suit and choker pearls she felt countryfied.

She felt she had been rather monosyllabic with Marie, had shown none of the spontaneous delight she ought to have done on meeting someone from one's childhood memories, so she made an effort.

"I hope you're coming down to Heatherleigh for the Christmas holidays, Marie?"

47

Muir answered for her.

"You'll be seeing her much sooner than that. Marie is to be in Oamaru for a few weeks very shortly."

Roberta pretended a pleasure she did not feel. What on earth was the matter with her?

When they said goodbye, Marie lifted a cool cheek to each of them. Muir wasn't in the least embarrassed as he kissed Marie, Roberta noticed.

"I won't say 'see you in Oamaru,' Marie, because I expect to be up here again before long," he said.

Marie waited till they were airborne, waving to them from the edge of the airstrip, then suddenly they could see her no more.

Roberta thought no more about air crashes, but somehow the joy had gone out of the day. And why was Marie coming to Oamaru? She wouldn't ask. . . .

October came in with plumes of purple and gold, and the lambing was nearly finished.

"Up in the foothills they'll not be started yet," said Muir, as he and Roberta rode around the sheep one morning. "At Hakataramea Valley they don't start till well into October, they're near the snowline there."

It had been a big month for Roberta. She had proved her worth at lambing time, and had spent long hours out of doors. Sometimes she and her grandfather rode out together, on the days when Muir could spend no time at Heatherleigh, and usually George went with them too. The old man was past that sort of work really, and so the two younger members of the family spared him all they could, making sure that he felt they relied on his longer experience, and that they were really just working under his orders. Old Robert told himself he was seeing they gained experience, but he was glad of their aid.

Roberta was no onlooker, and was entirely unself-conscious when helping with difficult births, no matter whom she was with.

Muir looked at her as she rose to her feet, and at the

newly-delivered lamb, yellow and wet, and laughed at her.

"It must be in the blood, Roberta."

"It is," she agreed, and wiped her hands on a piece of mutton-cloth. "Funny, isn't it? And Mother just loathed farm life. I wonder from whom she got her love of city life?"

"Some long-ago forebear, I suppose," said Muir, and quoted: "'No man is free who has a thousand ancestors.'"

"Burns?" queried Roberta, saucily.

"I do occasionally read other poets," said Muir, "and I've no idea who said that. I think we'd better take this one back home, Roberta, and put it under the lamp for a while."

There were boxes in the wash-house and on the back porch, with electric lamps attached for reviving weak lambs. It was much more efficient than clustering them around a fire, or putting them into a hot bath, and rubbing them vigorously, though one wet day earlier they had had all the lamps going, three fires lit, and the galvanised baths in use.

By November life at Heatherleigh had settled into much of its old atmosphere and routine. Roberta had managed to get a couple of girls to help Meg, fresh-faced girls, who, for a start, anyway, seemed to delight in their work and were charmed with their surroundings. They lived in the village and bicycled up to the big house each day.

Roberta's rooms over the stables saw her every day now, for a few hours, and as the household dropped into settled ways she began restoring the old stables under the clock tower to something of their former glory.

Grandfather had bought two ponies for the children, and Josephine and David were only too happy to help with the harness room. Old Robert had offered to buy Roberta a mount, but she had grown fond of Clancy, and scarcely a day passed that she was not in the saddle. She and George shared many rides. He and Grandfather were out together constantly, sometimes on horseback, but more often in the Land-rover they used so much on the estate.

During the winter months Grandy and the men had put in eight miles of rabbit-proof fencing around the wheat paddocks of Buchanan and Heatherleigh. Some of the fencing went uphill, and Roberta always marvelled at the difference of the pastures, as she gazed up the fenceline.

On one side, where the rabbits still had their burrows in between the rocks in the rougher parts, there was only a thin sole of greyish grass, while on the protected side the grass was emerald green, thick and spongy beneath one's feet. It was like seeing a two-tone ribbon in satin and glacé. But there was no doubt that the rabbit menace was fast disappearing.

Roberta was glad whenever she saw Grandy going off with George. It was good that there was someone of the younger generation of Heatherleighs to carry on ... but what a tragedy that the old man should have outlived his sons.

She had more time now to linger over the great flower-bowls and urns that graced so well the big rooms. Now, she put her head on one side as she regarded her handiwork in the drawing-room which she had opened up after many years in dust covers.

She filled a tall jar with delphiniums, pink and mauve and blue, with larkspur and cornflowers, and a low white trough she filled with candytuft and clarkia for the windowsill. She picked up another bowl and studied it. Perhaps some Shot Silk roses in here, or some of the Peace roses, flushed on their creamy petals with cerise?

George sauntered in.

Roberta said: "Oh, I thought you were with Grandy in the study."

George shook his head. "No, Muir's with him. Did it ever strike you, Roberta, how much Buchanan runs Heatherleigh? He's for ever interfering."

She had noticed the last few weeks how often George criticised Muir's methods, and she had been surprised to notice that she herself always wanted to rush to Muir's defence, however much she and Muir might spar personally.

She stopped dusting and said: "Muir's pretty sound in his judgements, though, George, and he knows this country far more intimately than you or I. He and Grandy have always

50

worked together. Muir does almost as much for the estate as he ever did, and I don't know how the place would have got on without him all these years when Grandfather carried on alone."

"That's as may be, but he does impose his will on the old man. He pretty well runs Heatherleigh, and I don't like it. I can't believe it's disinterested, or all in the sacred name of friendship. There's something behind it, though I don't know quite what. I wouldn't be surprised if Muir covets the place for himself. I think it's just as well you and I turned up."

Roberta ran her duster over a row of miniatures, then stopped and looked at them, changing the subject.

"Aren't these beautiful? Simply exquisite!"

"Mmm," said George, without enthusiasm. "Worth quite a bit, the old man told me."

Roberta said: "Daddy did one of me, and sent it to Grandy years ago. I asked him the other day where it was, and he just grunted and said: 'In my safe, I daresay.' I thought how odd it was when he had these really valuable ones out on the wall."

George's eye was following the progress of her lambswool duster.

"A real dust trap, that old chair, isn't it? And not at all comfortable to sit on."

It certainly wouldn't be. It had a heavily carved seat, and shell-like curved back, but it was a collector's piece and a thing of intricate beauty.

"When you think of the money it represents," said George, "it seem ridiculous to think of its being here, stuck in this Godforsaken place where no one ever sees it."

Anger flowed like a tide through Roberta. Heatherleigh ... Godforsaken...! She could understand that being said about some of the outback stations, days from anywhere, but – but Heatherleigh!

"*We* see it. Beauty is never wasted. Grandy's mother brought that chair out with her. It's part of Heatherleigh, and always has been."

51

She picked up a piece of Venetian glass, lovingly, carefully. It ought to be in one of the cabinets, but Grandy liked it on this ledge. He liked to have his treasures in use.

George laughed at her.

"Spitfire!" he said, catching hold of her wrists. He looked down at her. Her cheeks were flying red rags of rage. "You're very beautiful when you're in a rage, my dear Roberta. I must make you mad more often."

He bent towards her, his blue eyes alight with mischief. Roberta was still angry, and it made her angrier still to think she couldn't pull away because she had a priceless goblet in her hands. George knew it and took full advantage of it, and brought his mouth down on hers, hard, lingeringly.

Roberta stood perfectly still in his embrace, neither resisting nor responding, till George released her. She found she was shaking, and was annoyed to think she was. George might not take it for rage, but for tenderness. She put out a hand to a small table to steady herself, and sensed rather than saw that someone had passed the open door. Who?

She heard the firm tread, and knew it for Muir. Perhaps he was on his way back to the study with papers he had fetched for Grandy. Had he seen? She knew a sudden unaccountable dismay . . . how ridiculous – what did it matter to her if Muir had seen the embrace?

She put the goblet back where it belonged and said quietly but intensely: "Don't dare do such a thing again, George," and went from the room, picking up her secateurs.

There was a fine tree of Shot Silk roses outside the study. Through the open window she heard Grandy say: "I'm more than grateful for all you've done in the matter, lad. You'll not lose by it. I'll see to that. I wouldn't like to see the estate pass into the wrong hands . . . it's a fair legacy. It's meant so much to me."

"It means a lot to me, too, sir," came in Muir's tones. Roberta thought his voice held relief. "Then you'll do as I suggest and . . ."

Roberta became aware that she was eavesdropping and fled hastily, though quietly. She had heard enough, anyway, to convince her, however unwillingly, that George was right about Muir. It checked up with all Muir's antagonism when first she came; and the knowledge was bitter.

She took her empty basket to the stables and sped up the rough stairway to her studio. She dropped into the chair by the table, put her head on her arms and stayed there a long time.

So Muir did covet Heatherleigh. It hurt ... not the thought of Heatherleigh passing out of the family, but that Muir should do this. He had always seemed so much above anything insincere, seemed to have a fine scorn for the things that came to you without working hard for them: it cancelled out all her hero-worship of years ago, upset her sense of values.

At the moment Roberta simply couldn't bear it ... she hated the years that had so changed them all ... George, who hadn't quite stayed a kindred spirit ... George, who as a youngster had fired Roberta's imagination because he had been such a gentle knight ... oh, hadn't she been a romantic? And ... and Muir, who had been so stable, so unflinchingly honest, scheming to inherit one of the largest estates in Otago?

Roberta felt a hand on her shoulder, and looked up, unwillingly. Muir!

"What's the matter, Roberta?" he asked. His tone and his eyes were all concern.

"Nothing's the matter," she said tonelessly "Nothing *you* could help with. Go away, please."

Muir's answer to that was to pull up another chair and to sit down, his arm across her shoulders.

"Come on, little one. You aye told me what was bothering you when you were small. It mightn't be so bad put into words, and I might be able to help."

Roberta kept her head down. She had always found it hard to disguise her feelings. This was disarming ... the old, familiar tenderness back in Muir's voice. She must realise it was meant to be disarming, part of his policy to keep her from guessing what he was working for.

Controlled, she lifted her head.

"Will you please go, Muir? I rather resent this intrusion on my privacy."

He got up, strangely unresentful, but before he turned, said, "I'll be at Buchanan if you need me."

As he turned his back on her and went unhurriedly to the door, she had an almost overpowering desire to call him back to ask what was wrong between them, why he had altered so. . . . But the moment passed, and she was thankful she had resisted it.

He got halfway across the studio and came back.

"What now?" she asked impatiently.

"You won't be tempted to go bathing with George in the Pool of Darkness, will you? It's full of snags just now."

"No, I won't." Her tone was muffled and a little surprised.

"And – and—" Muir was unusually hesitant for him, "with having such little rain, the ground is terribly hard and slippery. Just be careful if you're out riding on the high ground. George is reckless."

"Thanks for the solicitude," she said mockingly.

He said: "You're rather important, Roberta, to all of us," and smiled. She didn't smile back. His words were enigmatic, as if something lay behind them. She was to remember them later. He stood there, holding her eyes, seemingly so much the old Muir he had been that she found it hard not to respond.

She got abruptly to her feet.

"Look, Muir, I've got work to do. I want to get some sketches away. The new models came in yesterday, and I'll have to get the drawings into Oamaru for the two-forty, so they can connect with the air-mail at Harewood Airport tomorrow."

She walked briefly to a long shelf where she kept goods for illustrating, and shook some miniature garments on to the bench out of their pink tissue wrappings. She gave a flick to unfold them, turned her back on Muir and began fastening a brassiere in white lace and nylon on a tiny model in front of her. This would get rid of him. She hooked it up over the pink plaster curves and expertly rolled down the tiny roll-on that matched it, slipped them over the neck and shoulders, turned them around, and tugged them into position to make a wrinkleless fit.

She then lifted over a half-finished sketch of a bride, and picked up a pencil. She said, over her shoulder,

"Goodbye, Muir. This is no place for you."

He laughed then, and came closer, putting a hand on her shoulder.

"You still won't tell me what was wrong?"

"Muir! Forget it. Can a woman not sit down and have a good cry once in a while to relieve her feelings, without having to explain why?"

He said shrewdly, "I'd not noticed any tears. If it's just a bit of temperament, it's all right, but—" He turned and went away.

Roberta got her illustrations done, caught the express with them by the skin of her teeth, putting double postage on and dropping them into the post box on the guard's van on the rear of the express.

When she got home David and Josephine were out of school, so the three of them cleaned the fowl houses and dug over the runs. The heavy work did Roberta good.

"I think you'll all need baths before dinner," said Meg, as they appeared before her, dirty and dishevelled. Roberta went upstairs and got thankfully into the soapy, scented water. She was too tired to think now.

Donald usually served the dinner Meg cooked. He loved the reversion to the old order of things. He and the maids had theirs in the kitchen, and in the main Meg and the children had theirs in their own rooms. That way Meg felt that she preserved the children's family life, and it kept them from overdoing things with old Mr. Heatherleigh. At his age children could be a nuisance. That was her idea, not his. The old man was always happier when there were more places set at the big table.

Roberta came downstairs in a soft green velvet housecoat, with a gold tinsel cord that tied about the waist, and fell to the hem of the full skirts.

George waited at the foot of the stairs and watched her come down, his eyes appreciative of the picture she made.

"How about an early bathe tomorrow morning, Roberta? The mornings are getting warmer now."

She shook her head. "No, thanks. I prefer bathing later in the day when the sun has been on the pools for a while."

"The sun shines early on the Pool of Darkness. It's the only time it does get the sun." He cocked his head and looked at her persuasively.

"Muir doesn't think we should go there to swim, George. It was flooded last winter, and it's full of snags."

"Muir!" exploded George. "Does he think we're still kids?"

Roberta pulled a face. She would like to have flouted Muir in this, but he knew the river and . . . and the habit of obedience to Muir died hard.

"He probably does, but I think he's right, just the same. Anyway, I'll not be coming. I'm woefully tired, that's why I'm in this housecoat. I'll go to bed early, and sleep late."

CHAPTER THREE

ROBERTA didn't sleep late. She awoke to find the early sunlight slanting across her pillow and birds stirring in their morning chorus.

It was too good a morning to stay in bed. It was wonderful what a difference a good night's sleep made . . . what was the line? – Oh, yes, "Sleep that knits up the ravelled sleave of care." True enough. Why, this morning she was certain that what she had overheard about the legacy would have some reasonable explanation.

It would be good to ride alone this morning, with no human contacts to cloud the sky. As she slipped out into the stableyard, the clock tower showed half-past four. She had the world to herself. Where should she go?

Clancy decided it for her, for, as always when left to herself, she turned towards the hills upriver. There was a narrow track that led away from the bridge, well away from all the other houses on the estate. The track was powdered white with limestone dust, as were most of these North Otago lanes. It led through clustering willows for the most part, and past great golden clumps of gorse and broom. A lark had mounted in the blue heavens, that already looked brassy with the promise of yet another burningly hot day.

From a red-flowering gum rose a *tui*'s song. Roberta checked Clancy to listen. There was magic in every note. As she rode on the bird flew out with a startled taffeta swish of wings, and flew to a tufty cabbage tree further away.

She breathed deeply now, and smelt a wave of sweetness on the early air. Up on the hillside the rabbits scuttled away, all part of the spirit of the morning. Roberta often felt guilty because she loved rabbits so much. It probably harked back to childhood days, and being brought up on Beatrix Potter. A pity they destroyed so much good grazing.

A hare broke cover and loped gracefully uphill, stopping out of sheer curiosity a few yards on, its long ears laid back, listening. As the track took a turn among the trees Roberta dropped Clancy to a walk. She had no desire to be swept off by an overhanging branch.

So it was that her hoofbeats were muffled as Clancy came to the edge of the clearing beyond which dipped the river into a wide, sunny pool, rock-edged.

As Roberta glanced across to the further edge of the pool, she checked Clancy, and remained where she was, in the shadow of the trees.

On a long, jutting arm of rock, poised for diving, was the figure of a man. There was a sudden flash of movement and Muir was cleaving the water. He came up in the centre of the pool, shaking the water out of his eyes.

He came to the rock again, clambered up, and stood there, water dripping off him. Even at that distance Roberta could see how copper-brown he was. She grinned to herself, remembering how young George had said: "I think he's a bit of a Red Indian, don't you, Rob?"

Roberta slipped off Clancy, and slid a hand down his nose. Muir's horse was probably tethered nearby and Clancy might whinny. Roberta didn't want to break the spell of this morning hour. All the artist in her rose to it . . . there was a poetry of movement here. . . .

Muir lifted his arms again for a dive and the muscles rippled under his skin like satin. Five, six times he dived.

All of a sudden Roberta had a curious sensation — no, two. One was that instinct was fighting against reason. Although everything seemed to point to it, Muir just couldn't be a schemer. The other . . . the other was so vivid it over-whelmed the first.

It seemed to Roberta that this had all happened before . . . this was a morning in the dawn of time, and the willows by the brook were really part of a primeval forest . . . this was her man, copper-coloured by the sun . . . her mate for all time.

The moment passed as quickly as it had come, and she

was ready to smile at the absurdity of it. She was Roberta O'More, watching Muir Buchanan swimming mother-naked in the Wainakarua, and he might not be pleased at that!

A smile of sheer mischief touched the corners of her eyes and mouth. Wouldn't it be fun to tease? She tethered Clancy to a tree and started to work her way quietly around the pool behind the trees, hoping the mare would not whinny.

When she came on to the arm of the rock, still quietly, the Scotsman had just surfaced. She sat down, tucked her legs under her neatly, and called demurely, "Good morning, Muir."

She saw him turn over in a flash, and stand shoulder-deep in the water. She had a hand up to her eyes, shading them from the sunlight that streamed directly at her, as if dazzled by it. Muir wouldn't be sure how long she had been there, and if she had noticed his lack of bathing shorts.

He waded cautiously to the edge of the rock, and clung to it, evidently glad of the deep water.

She said, guilelessly: "I think I'll come in, Muir. It looks lovely."

He said quickly: "No . . . I wouldn't if I were you. It's terribly cold in here this morning."

Roberta looked incredulous. "Cold? On a morning like this? Besides, it wouldn't matter to me . . . they say men feel the cold more than women."

She paused, then added: "But if you're cold, Muir, you'd better come up. Here. . . ." She reached a hand down to him.

Muir retreated further into the depths.

"N-No. Not just yet. I'll . . . have a few moments more."

Roberta trailed her fingers in the water.

"It's not a bit cold."

Muir said hopefully, "Well, duck off behind those trees and get into your bathing suit, Roberta, if you think it won't be too cold for you."

She could almost see him measuring the distance to where his clothes were, and calculating how long it would take him to get into them.

Her eyes danced, the green lights in them more noticeable than ever.

"Oh, I haven't got a suit, but from what I – er – noticed, I thought bathing togs weren't regarded as essential in this part of the world!"

Muir muttered something, and Roberta shouted with laughter.

"It's something to see you at a disadvantage, Muir Buchanan."

"Roberta O'More!" said the man sternly, "get away into that bush yonder while I get dressed, then I'll deal with you."

She took pity on him and went. After all, she had had her fun. He wasn't three minutes getting into his breeches and tartan shirt.

"Right," he called, and Roberta emerged from behind a huge-trunked blue-gum. She laughed as she came.

He stood there, hands on hips. She thought he looked grim. Then a reluctant grin broke up the severity.

"How long were you there?"

Roberta put a finger to her chin in a pretence at calculating.

"It might have been five minutes . . . it might have been ten. I came through over there." She pointed. "I watched you dive six times. You dive well, Muir."

He said reprovingly: "You ought to have coughed."

Her one dimple quivered, then she subdued it and said comfortingly and with gravity, "It's further away than it seems."

She looked up at him, serious now.

"It's the first time I've ever longed to model in clay, Muir. My medium has always been paper and pencil and brush, but to do justice to you, one would need substance under one's fingers to mould the strength and the muscle." Her fingers went out in a gesture as if they were cupping the clay. "I knew a sculptor in Sydney whose work I have always admired. I wish he'd been here."

Her tone was completely impersonal, as well it might be,

60

with the background of the artistic life she had known so long. Beauty and strength of form and figure would always have an appeal for her, but solely for its artistry. She might have been discussing a statue, not flesh and blood.

She was looking beyond him at the shimmering water, but suddenly was aware that he had made a movement. She looked up at him, a little alarmed, as he took a quick step towards her.

She put out a hand in some agitation. He caught that hand in one of his, and with the other arm drew her close. Roberta closed her eyes as his lips came down on hers, hard and compelling. Roberta had never before experienced an embrace like this, something that seemed to challenge her to be aware of him as a man.

She didn't know how long they stood there. When Muir did lift his mouth from hers, they drew apart a little, not looking at each other. Roberta was breathless. This, then, was the meaning of that moment at the other side of the pool. . . . She loved Muir, had always loved him. It would mean the same to him. You couldn't imagine Muir Buchanan with a taste for stray kisses. This was what had brought her from the other side of the world . . . not just the ties that bound her to Heatherleigh. Her heart was light as it had not been since she had first come home. Everything would be explained now. That instinctive movement of Muir's towards her had swept away all doubts.

She looked up, and caught a strange expression on Muir's face. Whatever it meant, dismay caught at her throat.

He laughed shortly, as if remembering something he did not want to remember, and said: "Well, if George can kiss you, so can I!"

She gazed at him, unable to believe his words, or his tone, or his look. Then the colour ran up into her face. She felt humiliated, hurt. She couldn't quite get her feelings under control. To be sure one moment of everything that life could mean . . . then to be cast down like this, sure of nothing any more. She was aware that her face was betraying too much of her feelings. She looked away from Muir's burning gaze.

61

across the pool to the shadowy woods beyond. One moment away from his eyes was sufficient. Roberta was herself again.

She achieved a chuckle, a maddeningly flippant chuckle.

"Yes, so he did," she said. "Life's far more amusing at Heatherleigh than I had thought it would be. Almost continental, in fact. You and George both have your moments, haven't you? It adds quite a spice to a rural existence!"

Muir made a movement towards her, as if he wanted to speak, then changed his mind.

Roberta said lightly: "I've not told anyone I'm out. I must be on my way. They might think I've eloped . . . like mother, like daughter, you know."

Muir said: "I've got Sally tethered over here. I'll get her and we'll ride back together."

Roberta was firm. "No, Muir. I'd rather be alone. I'll take the track through the woods. It will be quicker for you to go through the cutting. See you again, sometime."

She leapt lightly across the huge boulders till she came to the coarse, tussocky grass beyond, and reached Clancy who whickered softly in welcome. Roberta leaned her head against the mare, putting her cheek close to the warmth of her. So that kiss meant as little to Muir as that? Very well, Buchanan.

The incident might have resumed normal proportions as far as Roberta was concerned, but after breakfast Grandfather wanted to see her in the study. Roberta drained the last of her coffee and followed him in.

He went across to his safe and opened it. He took out an oval case, covered with rather shabby purple velvet, and came back to Roberta, who was sitting on the edge of his desk, swinging her breeched legs. He put the case in her hands.

"I want you to have these, lassie. They were your grandmother's."

"Oh, Grandy!" She opened the case. A string of milky-white pearls, perfectly matched, with a diamond clasp. A short, fascinating string.

62

She slipped off the desk and put her two warm hands about the old man's face, looked into his eyes, blinked her own to deal with the tears that had risen, and kissed him.

Grandy said slowly: "I'd always promised Ishbel a string of pearls. I used to think I'd get them as soon as ever my position was a little more secure . . . as soon as ever I was worth so much . . . when my flocks reached a certain total . . . as soon as Heatherleigh was a certain acreage.

"I had the chance of buying in five hundred acres towards the Dachshund", (Roberta knew where he meant, a long, low line of hills that from the Heatherleigh Arms looked very like a dachshund), "but just before the deal went through, Ishbel took diphtheria. We thought she wasn't going to pull through. But she did. The doctor battled through storm and wind and river and shingle and mud to get here, and opened her throat. I didn't buy the land . . . I suddenly realised the land is always here, if not mine, then someone else's. That it was a pity to be always wise with one's money, that there is a time for extravagance. Ishbel had a lovely throat, and she suited the pearls. They quite hid the scar of the tracheotomy. I'd like to think you wore them."

He clasped the pearls about Roberta's slim brown throat. They contrasted oddly with the open-necked green silk shirt and gabardine breeches.

Grandy said: "We always have a big ball here for the estate staff on New Year's Eve. You'll wear the necklace then, won't you?"

She nodded and said: "May I run into the hall and look in the mirror there, Grandy?"

He watched her from the doorway, smiling, his thoughts busy. She came back, slipped the pearls carefully into their place in the grooved lining, and gave him the case to replace in the safe.

Then, because Robert Heatherleigh knew full well that the years were creeping quickly on him now, and he had all of an old man's impatience to see his dearest dream come true, he turned from the safe and said:

"Were you riding with Buchanan this morning?"

She shook her head.

"No, but I met him by the river, up past Yellowstone Ford. Why?"

"Just that I'm delighted to see you and Muir such good friends. He's a fine one, Muir Buchanan. Just the man to carry this place on after I'm gone."

Roberta stood motionless. The sunlight from the curved window fell palely on her shining head. There was a silence.

She braced her shoulders a little, She moistened her suddenly dry lips.

"You mean – you mean—" Her voice trailed off.

Grandfather didn't seem to notice her dismay. He was simply pleased she had caught on so quickly.

"I mean I'd like nothing more than to know Muir Buchanan would keep on all the traditions of the Heatherleigh estate in the years to come."

Roberta's tone was cold.

"Why not George? After all, *he* is a Heatherleigh."

Roberta said sharply: "I wouldn't put Heatherleigh into George's hands."

"Why?"

"George would sell it. Land to George means so much an acre . . . a house so many thousands of pounds."

"Rubbish," said Roberta, crushing down the thought of George's appraisal of the family miniatures. "Have you forgotten how George, as a small boy, loved Heatherleigh? Don't you remember how when he was leaving he packed in his case a bit of the stone that had crumbled away from the west porch? Don't you?"

"Aye," said the old man. "But how much of the young George is there in the George of today? I find very little."

Roberta said hotly: "I think someone has prejudiced you against George."

She suddenly couldn't bear any more, and turned and flew from the room. Grandy heard her footsteps flying upstairs and the sharp bang of her door.

He shook his head philosophically.

"Very, very like Ishbel," he murmured to himself. Ishbel

had been given to sudden and inexplicable rages, had known fierce loyalties too, had championed lost causes. Roberta would soon find out she couldn't depend on George. Anyway, as far as Muir was concerned, he had dropped a hint in the right direction.

Upstairs, Roberta was thinking things out, sitting by her window and letting the cool breeze fan her hot cheeks. No doubt Grandfather and Muir had had a talk together. Very nice . . . all so simple. Marry Roberta, perhaps even take the name of Heatherleigh, produce a few sons, the eldest, of course, to be Robert, and . . . well, all that is mine is thine! Not bad for a man who had started off as a shepherd lad.

Perhaps Muir had had thoughts of inheriting Heatherleigh before Roberta had appeared on the scene. Poor Muir, George turning up must have given him a shock to start with. So he had prejudiced Grandy against George, then, when Muir got over his first resentment at her own return (as he seemed to have done), he decided it need not upset his plans at all. He would acquire a wife and an estate. Very masterly. She suddenly remembered Muir's words to her when he had warned her against bathing in the river and riding on slippery hillsides . . . "You're rather important, Roberta, to all of us." Yes, of course, a pawn in their game!

Roberta burned inwardly at the recollection of her feelings beside the pool, that moment of certainty, when she thought she had recognised Muir as her man . . . the kiss, then Muir's voice, harsh and grim. "If George can kiss you, so can I!"

It must have disconcerted Muir to see her fast in George's arms . . . that would never do. It wasn't masculine jealousy that had prompted that remark, it wasn't even a sneer, it was simply chagrin that George had got in first.

Roberta looked across at the hill that hid Buchanan. For two pins she'd march over there and confront Muir, and turn him down there and then. The hot thoughts coursed through her mind. But stay . . . wouldn't it be a little difficult turning down a man who'd not yet proposed . . . who was only planning to? It might, at that.

An idea shot through Roberta's mind. Yes, Grandy probably would not tell Muir he had been trying to further his cause. Why not let him think she was attracted to him? At the thought of his chagrin, when, after leading him to believe all was well, she turned him down, an impish smile touched the bitter curves of Roberta's mouth.

Her eye wandered to the low stone wall where she had sat just a few weeks ago, and Muir had held her by the arms in the moonlight. Yes, she could easily engineer little incidents like that. It would be fun . . . or would it? It would hurt . . . no, she wouldn't *let* it hurt. She would pay Muir Buchanan in his own coin, and at the end of it all she would be as heartwhole as when she had come to Heatherleigh.

Muir came over and had after-dinner coffee with them the following evening. Roberta was lying on the hearthrug with David and Josephine, doing a jigsaw. She decided that this could be where her campaign might well begin. She said, popping in a weirdly shaped section of cloudy sky:

"There! I think you'll manage the rest yourselves, youngsters. I want Muir to have a look at Clancy's hoof."

To Muir, as they crossed to the stables, she said: "I thought it seemed a bit tender today. I couldn't see a thing, but you might know better than I what to look for."

He couldn't find anything, which wasn't surprising, since Roberta had invented the whole thing. She professed herself relieved that it was nothing serious, then invited Muir up to her studio. He had not seen it since the morning he had found her with her head on her arms.

The room was full of the purple shadows of twilight. A peach branch, showing young fruit now among the leaves, tapped at the half-open window.

"In autumn," said Roberta, "I shall be able to lean out and pick myself a peach whenever I feel like it."

Muir nodded. He had planted that peach below the window when these quarters were his.

"I rather like to think of you working away up here, where I used to work, polishing harness and reading all I could of agriculture, and sheep-farming . . . yes, and Burns."

66

Roberta had put down a square of cool-looking matting on the floor, and beside the fireplace was a painted bookshelf with books on art. On it stood a ginger jar filled with blood-red peonies. She glanced through the casement.

"Oh, look, there's the evening star."

They turned to the deep stone windowsill, set in the thick wall. Roberta pushed the double casement open wide.

It was a perfect view of Heatherleigh, the sweeping roofs and gables, the odd corners that jutted out. Around the curved windows of the study, wistaria was in full bloom. Over to the east, tall poplars and cypresses were tapering shadows, thick and dark. Beneath them rose the scents of the garden.

There was just room for their elbows on the sill and it brought them close together. Roberta turned a little, deliberately, so that her hair brushed against Muir's cheek. She was vibrantly aware of him, and angry that she should be. She subdued her feelings, telling herself it was all a means to an end, and set herself to the task in hand. She gave an appreciative sniff.

"That's nice tobacco you smoke, Muir. I can smell it on your jacket." She moved away, tantalisingly distant.

Muir's eyes went to the two chairs by the hearth, the cones and blue-gum logs piled for the lighting, the glass-fronted cupboard that held china and a tea caddy; the low table between the chairs, the open magazine on it.

"You spend quite a lot of time up here, Roberta?"

She nodded. "Yes, I'm fond of my own company. I like people, but I have to get away by myself at times."

He smiled at her.

"I read the other day that a person who is not afraid to be alone has good thoughts for company." He came nearer her. "What sort of thoughts keep you company, Roberta?"

She looked away. She mustn't let his — his niceness — lull her into thinking he wasn't hard and calculating.

She shrugged her shoulders.

"A motley lot of thoughts, like most, I suppose."

His hands came out to grip her shoulders.

"Am I ever in them, Roberta?" His eyes searched hers. The green lights danced in them.

"Yes," she admitted easily. "You were in them a lot today."

His eyes were warm. She added, "I was so worried about Clancy's hoof, you see."

Muir chuckled, gave her a little shake, let her go. He said: "You know there's a Shakespeare play on in Dunedin . . . the New Zealand Players? Would you like to go on Thursday night?"

Roberta gazed at him.

"Go eighty miles, just for the evening, and back?"

"We often do," he said. (Oh, yes, he and Marie had gone to plays, before now.) "You could feel too isolated in the country if you let distance keep you from the things the country can't supply. I sometimes go for a good film if I think it won't come to Oamaru eventually. We can leave here just after six. I'll milk early. Henk is going over to his cousin's birthday party, and he can stay the night."

"All right," said Roberta.

Muir went on: "We'll have dinner together first, at my place. I'll prove to you that I can cook quite a good dinner. No frills, of course, and it will have to be early. And listen . . . no quixotic impulses about asking George and Meg along too, see?"

Roberta agreed docilely. No, it wasn't part of her plan to have the others tagging along, she thought.

"So tomorrow night you'd better have an early night, my lass, because it will be late the next night."

"Don't you just love bossing people around, Muir Buchanan!" Roberta sounded like a cross child. "I'll do nothing of the kind. George and I are going to the Derwents' for the evening."

Muir was supposed to look aggrieved about that, but he was disconcertingly indifferent. He stayed a while longer, then made his way down the stone stairway on to the cobbled bricks of the courtyard. She heard him out on the metalled road that led to Buchanan, whistling: *"Pipes of the misty moorland, voices of glens and hills. . . ."*

Muir Buchanan appeared to be pleased with himself . . . and well he might be, for a little time.

It was a relief to go out with George the next night. Nice not to have to pretend, not to have to repress any traitorous gladness at hearing Muir's voice, his step.

Good, too, to find the Derwents unchanged. Lester and Donald were still home, Nessie married, but as she lived just the other side of the Arms, was home for the evening with her husband, Ian Gordon. Mrs. Derwent put on as large a supper as of yore.

Roberta sparkled. It was lovely to find that that month so long ago had meant just as much to these folk as it had to her. There were no doubts here to nag and tantalise. You could be sure of the affection and friendliness you met here. No one had a motive for anything.

Roberta had her car, but George was driving it. They dropped Ian and Nessie on the way home, then drove slowly. In the bright moonlight, the track to the estate, metalled with the white Ngpara gravel, showed like a silver ribbon winding through velvety shadows where trees clustered close, and it dipped over the innumerable bridges where the streams crossed the roads.

They ran Roberta's little car in beside the big De Soto, the station wagon and the Land-rover, and locked the garage doors.

Silently they walked across the courtyard and over the side lawn to the little curved door. George opened it with his latch-key, locked it from the inside again, and shot the bolt home.

He turned to Roberta. The moonlight slanted in through the fan-shaped leaded casement at the far side of the door, a shaft falling across George and turning his hair to steel. The pale, unearthly light made his face look young and defenceless. George as he used to be.

69

He said: "You don't hold me at a distance like the others here do."

She said warmly: "Of course not. Why should I?"

George reached out his hands and drew her to him.

Roberta hesitated. She didn't like to repulse George when he evidently felt lonely and shut out, but she didn't want him to kiss her.

She drew back. "I'm tired, George," she said breathlessly.

George laughed. "You're a little puritan, aren't you, Roberta? In spite of your upbringing!"

She flashed around on him. "George! Don't *you* be like all the rest, imagine all sorts of orgies in artists' quarters, and whatnot. Daddy and Mother never loved anyone but each other, and they were strict with me. I don't go in for casual lovemaking."

George said, twinkling, "I didn't mean it to be casual, Roberta." He gripped her more firmly. "I'm dead serious about this. You know how I feel about you, don't you?"

He wasn't prepared for Roberta's quick twist out of his grasp, and her sudden flight up the side stairs. He stood for a moment, nonplussed, then laughed to himself, not ill pleased. She wasn't as sophisticated as she appeared on the surface. On the whole, it had been a pleasant evening.

Upstairs, Roberta was frowning as she kicked off her shoes . . . she would have to be careful, she mustn't hurt George. Life could certainly be difficult. She couldn't play George off against Muir if George's heart was going to be involved.

Tomorrow's outing was evidently going to be the first step in Muir's courting . . . the courting that was so deliberate and cold-blooded, a means to an end.

Roberta slid into a green frilly nightgown, and sprang into bed, burying her face in the pillow. Oh, Muir . . . Muir!

CHAPTER FOUR

At lunchtime the next day, Grandy told Roberta she would be lucky if Muir was able to get to the theatre that night.

"He's had quite a morning. He suffered from the power failure too, of course, and had to milk his cows by hand, but our troubles stopped there, Buchanan's didn't. A stoat had got into his large pen of seven-week-old pullets and accounted for more than a score of them. Then a mechanical fault developed in the separator, and by the time he got that fixed the lamb buyer arrived."

"That was early, wasn't it?" asked Roberta.

"Aye. I gather Muir made that plain to him, but he happened to be in the district and wanted a look around. It's all set Buchanan back, so don't kick up a fuss, if you miss your theatre trip, lassie."

Roberta was indignant. "I'm not likely to. We can go another time. I know the work of the place must go on."

But she was inwardly disappointed just the same. She wanted to begin her plan without delay, and – well, there were times when she longed for bright lights as a little welcome relief.

At one o'clock she was called to the phone. It was Muir. She prepared for disappointment.

His voice came across to her.

"I've been held up and it's going to be a busy afternoon. I've not been around the sheep yet, and I daren't go out tonight without a look-over. You'd better stay home for dinner. I'll be over at six just the same. McGregor's going to see to the night's milking."

No doubt Roberta ought to have offered to go round the sheep for him, but she didn't. She laughed.

"Robbie said it well, Muir, didn't he? ... *'the best-laid plans o' mice and men ...'* What did you say? ... You shouldn't, you know, over the phone. You can be prosecuted

71

for that! All right, I'll tell Meg I'll not be out for dinner after all. I hope all your troubles are over now. See you at six." She hung up and went in search of Meg, who was mending linen.

"I'm going over to Buchanan now." She laughed. "I'll cook his dinner for him ... he's an exasperatingly self-sufficient creature. It will do him good to find a woman necessary after all."

The mess she found Buchanan in afforded Roberta a good deal of satisfaction ... the breakfast and lunch dishes piled up on the bench, the unswept kitchen floor, a pan of burnt porridge soaking in the sink, a dirty rim around the washbasin, towels that needed airing, the tousled, unmade beds, and ... curled up in the middle of Muir's, a blissful nose between paws that rested on his pyjamas ... Doss, Muir's old spaniel!

She looked up guiltily as Roberta came in, as one who knew her watchdog days were over. Roberta gave her an indulgent smack on her hindquarters and remarked:

"It serves your master right if he can't sleep tonight for fleas."

Doss ambled out through the hall and flopped with an audible sigh on the back porch mat. Roberta wasted no time. She found a delectable leg of mutton in the refrigerator, and a golden yellow pumpkin in the vegetable safe. She switched on the electric stove, sorted out baking dishes and basting spoons, and soon the meat was sizzling.

Out went the mats and off went the bedclothes. Henk rushed in on his way from school, accepted gratefully the hot cheese scone Roberta buttered for him, drank a glass of milk, conscientiously fed the fowls, washed himself sketchily, and showed Roberta the doll's bed he and Muir had made for small cousin Yetti, before departing. He promised not to tell Muir Roberta was getting the dinner if he happened to meet him.

When Roberta was dusting the bedside table in Muir's bedroom she noticed that some papers were sticking out of the shallow drawer in it. To get them in she had to pull the drawer right open.

It stuck fast. She gave a sudden jerk, and the whole thing fell out, spilling the contents on to the carpet. Roberta gave an annoyed exclamation, and knelt to retrieve them. The usual conglomeration of articles . . . studs and notebooks, a couple of receipts, some bright-coloured golf tees, three or four letters.

Under the letters she found it . . . the miniature of herself that her father had painted and which Grandy had said was locked in his safe. It was a good likeness of her. Stephen had painted his daughter in an amber ball dress with a high Tudor collar, latticed with pearls, that reared up behind her small head. The thick hair was brushed smoothly back from her brow, and belled around in a soft, curving line behind her ears. The lopsided dimple was in evidence.

It had been a labour of love . . . and here it was in Muir Buchanan's bedroom . . . Muir who only desired her because she could bring him Heatherleigh. She caught her full, passionate lower lip between her teeth. If only . . . if only he had had her picture there because he liked to look at it before he went to sleep . . . if only . . . ! But no — she could imagine Grandy, so pleased because his plans seemed to be going ahead so well, just like a well-thought-out game of chess, going over to his safe and getting out the miniature for Muir. It had probably embarrassed Muir and he had just dropped it into the first place he thought of.

Roberta squared her shoulders. She was playing a game too, a deep one, and wishing and dreaming had no part in it. She must go back to the kitchen, for Muir mightn't have much time to spare. The water in the cistern was boiling, so he could shave and bath. She saw the potatoes were turning a rich golden brown, popped the bundle of asparagus into boiling salted water, and began melting butter for the Dutch sauce to go over it.

She was glad there was a refectory table in the dining-room, and that Muir had some good crystal and silver. The garden was abloom with roses now. She put half a dozen full blown yellow ones into a low pottery bowl, and picked delphiniums and larkspur for a tall vase on the sideboard.

She was just taking the beautifully browned joint out of the oven as Muir came through the door. He got two steps in and halted from sheer surprise. Here was Roberta in a yellow linen dress, crisp and fresh, covered with an adequate-sized apron of brown checked gingham, a piece of brown ribbon tying back her hair, her cheeks flushed from bending over the stove.

"Well!" he said, as she carefully set the roasting dish on newspaper spread out on the table. A most appetising smell rose up to him, making him realise how famished he was.

She looked up, and the provocative dimple appeared.

"This is all," she announced, "to impress you with your own inadequacy."

He laughed. "You win." He tweaked the ear nearest him as he leaned against the table and watched her deftly skewer the joint with a carving fork and lift it on to the warm ashet.

"If you're thirsty," she told him crisply, "there's something cool in the fridge." He was. Roberta took out a pitcher full of orange and grapefruit juice, and after half filling a tumbler with it, added soda from a siphon she had brought from Heatherleigh.

"The kettle's boiling for your shave. You haven't got too much time to spare. I've hunted out what I imagine are your clean things . . . they're on the stool in the bathroom."

Muir looked back at her over his shoulder as he went out of the kitchen door.

"Did I only imagine it, or did you really tell me the other night that I liked bossing people? And I don't need the kettle, thanks. I use an electric razor."

Roberta drained off the fat, set the residue on the stove to brown for the gravy, whipped the boiled potatoes lightly, drained the pumpkin and broad beans, and placed them in their respective dishes. She took the mint sauce out of the refrigerator, and added vinegar. She could hear Muir singing "Lassie, will ye lo'e me" as he showered.

He came out of the bathroom and into his bedroom,

where the transformation from the disorder he had left this morning came as a surprise. The small jar of roses on the sill, the folded clothes, the shining furniture . . . and on his bed, spread widely, a gossamer gown of green with satin stripes embossed upon it. A matching slip, mostly lace and frills, lay beside it, and on the carpet stood a pair of extravagantly high-heeled gold sandals. He put out a hand and fingered the slip curiously yet carefully, smiling to himself. He went across to his wardrobe.

Roberta heard him call, and came in to him.

"Tie this blamed thing for me, will you?"

She obliged, wishing she could be less conscious of his nearness. He was breathtakingly handsome in these clothes. Strange, because she had thought he would look most at home in his breeches.

She tied the tie three times before she got it right, her hands were shaking so. She stepped back at last, put her head on one side, and said: "Yes, it will do."

"Thank you for making my bed," said Muir gravely.

She laughed. "I even rescued your precious Robbie Burns from where it lay face down on the floor."

"Robbie had a poem that might well fit this occasion," said Muir. "Do you know it? *'The lass that made the bed for me.'*" His dark eyes looked mischievous.

Roberta said hastily: "Now, Muir Buchanan! I'm not sure I altogether approve of Robbie Burns . . . in some ways he wasn't a very nice man!"

Muir put back his head and shouted with laughter. "Oh, Roberta!" he said. "And you knowing the artist quarter in Paris. No one would think it. You sound like a Victorian."

Roberta ignored that. "Come, or the dinner will spoil." She looked at Muir's magnificence and said ruefully: "I should have dressed for dinner too, to do you justice, but someone must wash the dishes."

After dinner Roberta said, "We'll have our coffee after I get changed. Will you switch it on again? It's in the percolator. I'll go and get ready. There are cheese scones in the green tin."

She was ready in an incredibly short time, and out again in the squirrel coat her grandfather had bought her. It was open over the full, flimsy skirts. The bodice had a scooped-out neckline, simply bound, and above it were Ishbel Heatherleigh's pearls. There were pearl bubbles at her ears, and her hair curled softly about them.

As they drove away they could hear the distant thrum of milking machines, and up in the home paddock a calf bawled disconsolately. As they swung on to the Main South Road, the peace of the evening seemed to descend upon Roberta. She leaned back against the seat and relaxed. For just this one night she would pretend this was real . . . that Muir loved her, not as a Heatherleigh, but because he couldn't help it.

Meanwhile the lovely road stretched out before them. There was no need to keep up a flow of small talk with Muir. The miles slipped by, and soon they were climbing the Kilmog.

Muir handled his car well, lovingly, even as he handled his horses. She turned her head a little, and studied him, covertly. The lean, hard jaws, the deep graven lines each side of his mouth, the jutting nose, the heavy brows, the eyes and mouth that could be such stern features, yet so meltingly tender at times.

"Well?" asked Muir, not taking his eyes from the road. "Weatherbeaten, aren't I?" Roberta almost jumped. She had thought him absorbed in the bends of the road.

She said hastily: "I was thinking how well you drive." She saw his mouth twitch, and knew he was not deceived. In fact he was probably pleased that she should regard him so closely.

He said: "You need the right companion for Shakespeare. Not someone who rustles chocolate papers in the tensest scenes."

Roberta laughed and continued: "Or wants icecream in the interval."

He said: "For instance, I should never dream of taking anyone who had no appreciation of the play to see *Othello*."

Roberta understood that. *Othello* was out of this world.

She couldn't help what she said next; it said itself for her.

"Have you ever taken Marie to see *Othello*?"

There was a long pause.

Then . . . "No," said Muir. "I went by myself to see it, the other year, when Anthony Quayle played it . . . an unforgettable experience." He shot a curious look at her. Roberta kept her colour down with an effort.

They swung into the Octagon with five minutes to spare, found a parking place in an incredibly short time, and soon were in the dress circle.

There was a magical, breathless quality about the whole evening. Roberta felt she should pinch herself to make sure she wasn't dreaming it all . . . she was here, with her grandfather's one-time shepherd, and he was as much at home in this sort of gathering as she was herself. Hitherto she had thought of him against a background of hills and sheep, drafting pens and harvesters.

Here there was an air of distinction about him. As the play progressed she realised there wasn't one subtle point, one minor sally he missed. . . .

They came out into the Octagon, and as they passed Burn's statue, Muir lifted a hand in laughing salute to the poet.

"You *are* absurd, Muir Buchanan," said Roberta.

Muir swung the car down Stuart Street and around Moray Place.

"I want to take you past First Church," he said. It was floodlit and beautiful, the home of Presbyterianism here in the southern hemisphere.

"I'll bring you down for an evening service some Sunday night," said Muir. "You know, don't you, that this was the church where Thomas Burns the nephew of the poet ministered. I know the present minister very well. We might get an invitation to supper in the manse. In the study, the shelves are edged with a beading made from Thomas Burns' study shelves."

Roberta had a sudden vision of Muir running his fingers reverently along the beading . . . homage to the poet. She had

77

a sudden impish thought, too . . . she wondered if Thomas had altogether appreciated being the nephew of Robert?

She said: 'What a lovely idea to have the church floodlit.'

Muir nodded. "I was once in a position to appreciate it even more. . . . I was in hospital, and in great pain. The ward I was in faced this way, and by raising myself just a little through the sleepless hours, I could see the steeple, as bright as day. It made me think of *The church her watch is keeping*. . . . It lessened the loneliness."

It was strange to think of Muir ever being lonely.

They came into Princess Street, parked and climbed the stairs to the Savoy. Roberta admitted it was good, after weeks on the estate, to be in the midst of bright lights and gaiety once more. Muir nodded. "We all need variety," he agreed.

Back in the car, Muir fished up a tartan rug for Roberta and tucked it carefully around her. They set off for the quiet hills above the dreaming peninsula. When they had left Cargill and the Kilmog behind, Muir's hand sought hers.

"Tired, little one? You're quiet."

"No . . . but on hills like that it's hardly fair to chatter to the driver. No, I feel as wide awake as if the night was still young, but it can't be. Some hours just fly, don't they, Muir?"

He smiled. "The happy hours do."

"Yes."

"Then they have been happy . . . for you too?"

She looked up, still playing a part and finding it easy to play, too easy. . . . Be careful, Roberta.

"But of course," she said. His hand tightened in answer.

"Sometimes we make ourselves slaves to time, on the land. Of course certain things must be done at fixed times, but occasionally I rebel, Roberta."

"Do you? Oh, Muir, look at that!"

She sat bolt upright in her eagerness. The road curved down to the shore here, and out beyond the low dunes, the headlights had lit up tumbling ranks of surf breaking in silver-white spray beneath the moon.

She sighed. "Just a glimpse of unearthly beauty . then we flash on. Sometimes I regret the pace we live at."

Muir slackened speed. He ran the car on to the grassy verge bordering the dunes.

"I told you I rebelled occasionally. We'll watch this for a while."

Roberta said: "I feel guilty. You have to be up so early, Muir."

He shrugged, looking down at her.

"All I'll lose is sleep . . . it's worth a little sleep to do as one pleases sometimes. Otherwise the loveliest things of life, things like this, get crowded out."

He continued to regard her. Roberta thought how much easier it would have been had she not known he was doing this for a purpose . . . building up atmosphere. The bitter-sweetness of it threatened to overwhelm her.

She said breathlessly: "But you're supposed to be looking at the moon, Muir Buchanan."

He laughed. "Aye, so I am. All right, Roberta O'More, let's look at it outside."

They walked along the bank till they were right opposite the track made by the moon across the sable waters. There was a warm, soft quality about the night, a gentle, fragrant balm.

Roberta's coat was open. The breeze from the Pacific blew the flimsy dress against her, outlining her young, slim grace. She was looking out to sea, lips parted, eyes feasting on the beauty of the night. Muir's eyes were on her loveliness of form and feature. She turned, catching him at it.

He said: "A Parisian gown, here under the Southern Cross."

Roberta said: "I've not seen anything lovelier than this, in all the lands I've lived in."

He laughed. "You're a real Maorilander, aren't you, Roberta, in spite of having lived all over the world and being an Australian to begin with?"

"It's easy to love New Zealand . . . and especially Heatherleigh — that's why I came back," said Roberta.

"Yes, it ought to be easy to love Heatherleigh," said Muir, and there was something dry in his tone, something Roberta didn't understand at all. In an instant the barrier was up between them again. She must guard against moments like some of the moments of tonight, when Muir had seemed so much like his old self that he had nearly disarmed her. In silence they drove on. By the time they reached home, Roberta had control of herself. She decided to carry on as she had planned.

It was three o'clock in the morning when they came to the arched side door. Had it been George she had been out with, Grandy would have been anxious, she supposed. But with Muir he felt she was safe. The orchard trees dappled the oaken wood of the door with a pattern of shadow. They stood for an irresolute moment, then Muir said: "Have you your key, Roberta?"

She took it out of the small evening bag she carried and gave it to him. He unlocked the door, and stepped with her into the friendly darkness of the study. A shaft of moonlight came through the window and they moved into it.

"I'm glad it was *Twelfth Night* we saw," said Muir. "It has a happy ending. I liked that line when the Duke said to Viola:

> *'Give me thy hand:*
> *And let me see thee in thy woman's garb.'* "

He smiled down at her. "I see you a lot in slacks and breeches . . . you'd make a good Viola, Roberta . . . but — I like you best in your woman's garb."

Oh . . . he was trying to recapture the atmosphere of the early evening. She smiled to herself, moved against him deliberately. He wasn't proof against her sudden nearness and the next moment she was caught hard against him, his lips on hers. Roberta was telling herself it didn't mean a thing to her . . . it was just part of the plan, getting Muir to the stage where she would turn him down. Her thoughts faltered for a moment. If only it hadn't been deliberate, if only this could have been part of an irresistible moment for them both, sweet as the summer night itself, with the promise of other delights to come. She drew back as far as she could, in his arms.

"I'll let you go in a minute," he said. "Don't strain away from me, small Roberta. I want to ask you something."

"Yes?" she said, in a breath scarcely above a whisper. Was this her moment of triumph? Oh, but it was coming too quickly . . . she wanted to play with Muir a little longer . . . *only* because it would make final triumph the sweeter, of course.

"Promise me you won't trust George too much?" Muir said.

Roberta felt as if she had missed a step in the dark. It took her time to marshal her thoughts.

She said: "That's not a thing anyone can promise, Muir. You either trust people or you don't."

"Do you trust him?" Muir insisted.

Roberta laughed, a strange, hard laugh. "Is there any trust at all in the atmosphere of Heatherleigh these days? Years ago we had such comradeship . . . our words mirrored our thoughts, but now they conceal them."

"That's tantamount to saying you don't trust George."

"Is it?" Her voice sounded weary. "I've junketed about the world a lot, fended for myself. Perhaps I don't trust anyone easily."

She turned in his embrace and switched on the light. Any magic the night might have had fled with the friendly darkness.

She couldn't tell much from his tone as he bade her a curt goodnight – except that she was sure there was no regret in it, and possibly some relief. She knew a relief herself that the night had ended, though it had had its moments of enchantment. She ran up the stairs in the deep silence of the sleeping house without a backward look. She switched on her light and contemplated her reflection in the mirror . . . eyes bright with pain, and a white, strained face . . . not easy to keep up, this game. And of course Muir was playing a part too. No wonder there had been relief in his tone.

CHAPTER FIVE

MUIR had asked Roberta to dine with him at the Heatherleigh Arms.

"To dine, if not to wine," he had said, with a whimsical lift of his eyebrows.

Part of North Otago was "dry", a no-licence area. There hadn't been a licensed hotel in the district for years. The nearest hotel with a bar was Georgetown, west of Oamaru, and there were no licensed hotels in Oamaru either.

Roberta didn't know what she thought about this . . . whether or not this was the answer to an international problem, and the ever-increasing menace of death on the roads, but she had to admit she had never seen a drunken man on the roads in North Otago, or in the town.

Heatherleigh Arms itself was unique, much more like an English inn than most New Zealand hotels. That was Robert Heatherleigh's doing. He owned the hotel and it was run and managed by a Mrs. Crossman, a capable, widowed Englishwoman.

It was not the usual two-storeyed wooden building, squat and square, rising direct from the shingle road, but was of limestone, wide and low, with a many-gabled roof of orange tiles, diamond-paned casement windows, and with terraces and rock gardens a blaze of colour before it, and the trees that bordered the river making a background of green behind it.

Robert Heatherleigh had spent a great deal of money on it, bestowing just the right atmosphere, years before it ever made a profit. Even now, all the profits went back into the hotel, improving the grounds, keeping up an excellent golf course, and the balance providing other amenities for the village.

"I want to have some place where the men of the community can gather and enjoy each other's company," he had said. So the parlour was a wide room, beamed and panelled. There was a good deal of brass and pewter about it, hunting prints, and colourful reproductions of long-ago artists who had painted the hazards of New Zealand's coaching days, when Cobb and Co. ran coaches to Dunedin over the old Horse Range route.

The fishing was excellent, the road tar-sealed most of the way into Oamaru, and Heatherleigh was far enough off the beaten track never to have lost its Sleepy Hollow air.

It was an excellent dinner. The salmon was perfect, the duck melted in the mouth, the sweets and the savoury all they should be. The dining-room was almost full, but Muir and Roberta had a secluded corner table looking out on to the rose gardens that sloped down to the river.

Over to the east there was a patch of native bush, starred now with clematis, the starry blossoms glimmering palely in the gathering dusk.

Roberta's eyes were on the garden, but Muir's were on her. She was wearing a long amber silk dress tonight, dull and rich, and against her throat gleamed the iridescent green and blue of a *paua* shell necklace set in silver links.

Muir had given it to her when he called for her, taking her out of the big hall into the study. He was very free of her grandfather's study, Roberta thought.

He had brought the necklace out of a jeweller's box. It had caught the light and reflected it back in a dozen differing rainbow gleams. Roberta had exclaimed with delight.

Muir had said, simply: "I gathered the *pauas* myself on Shelly Beach at the end of the cliff path that runs around Cape Wanbrow, and had them buffed and set in Christchurch. That's what I ran up there for last week."

He touched the centre, larger piece.

"I've had that shell thirteen years, Roberta. You won't remember, I suppose. You found it on the rocks at All Day Bay. You had a little box full of treasures, all those coloured stones you collected at the shore where the Awamoa Creek runs into the Pacific, a couple of fossils that the workmen gave you when I took you and George up to the stone quarry at Weston, and the moa bone that had been unearthed at the lime works.

When your mother decided they would make the luggage too heavy I took them over to my quarters."

Roberta felt the sudden prick of tears behind her lids. It had been one of the tragedies of childhood that she couldn't take these mementoes with her. Mother had been right, of course. It was absurd to think of carrying shells and pebbles across the world, but—

She remembered the day at All Day Bay, a clear autumn day, with the tussocks on the cliff-top blowing silver in the nor'west wind. Low tide, and all the treasures of rock pools beneath the cliffs, a stretch of beach that later she was to compare with the Cornish coast, with long reefs of treacherous kelp running out to sea, and jagged rocks. They had gone through an arch that was filled with water at high tide, to a little sandy cove, and Roberta had found the *paua* shell.

"Do you spell it p-a-h-w-a-h, Muir?" she had asked, and he had laughed at her and the next day had given her a Maori dictionary.

Roberta looked up into Muir's face, and in spite of her distrust of him, her heart softened. Gestures like this, that belonged to the Muir of yesterday, were wellnigh irresistible.

She put out her hands to him impulsively.

"You couldn't have given me anything I'd love more," she said, with shining eyes.

Muir had turned her around and clasped them about her throat. Her flesh was warm against his hard fingers. His hands slipped down to her waist, holding her against him. He put his cheek against her hair.

The door opened and in came Robert. Roberta, released, went scarlet. Muir was not in the least embarrassed, but then that weatherbeaten, hawklike face rarely betrayed emotion.

To gauge Muir's feelings you had to listen for the undertones of his voice, that softened immeasurably when he was moved, and there was always a hint of Scots burr and dialect then.

Now, at the dinner table, Roberta leaned her chin on her hands, then unclasped one to touch her necklace fleetingly.

"I'm dying to look at it again," she confessed. "With a necklace you get as much pleasure out of the feel of it against your skin as looking at it in a mirror. This has such a cool feel, I'm conscious of it all the time. It's like a touch of the ocean itself."

She turned to look down in the garden again, because there was something in Muir's gaze that she wanted to respond to . . . she must, she *must* remember she was only playing a part. But she was finding it difficult tonight. All of her cried out to meet Muir in his lovemaking, every instinct urged her to trust him, yet she must let reason take over, reason and common sense, for she had the evidence of her ears to convince her, that he courted her for Heatherleigh.

I'll admit, she thought to herself, that he finds me attractive. How pleasant for him! If he had detested me, I wonder would the estate have gilded the pill enough? But as it is, he finds it easy to court me. . . . He's not exactly marrying for money . . . or at least, land . . . but where land is. . . .

She looked down and saw George, loitering by the side door.

This was the only window that looked this way. She wondered idly why he hadn't come in from the front. The door opened and one of the girls from the staff came out. She said something to George, with a quick glance over her shoulder. He looked at his watch, said something, nodded, then strolled off down a little track that led down to the river. It looked like an assignation. The girl would slip out after her work was done, she supposed.

It didn't matter, of course, but Roberta wished it hadn't been that particular girl, for she didn't have a very good name in the village, and George had been going out a lot at night, very late. She was glad Muir hadn't seen him, or he would have looked at her with an I-told-you-so look, and warned her again about trusting George.

Muir said: "We'll go into the parlour for a little while, Roberta, and have a game of darts, then I'll take you over to Buchanan. With Henk staying at Heatherleigh with David for the night, we can have the place to ourselves."

Muir was furthering his suit quite well, wasn't he, said Roberta's mind to Roberta's heart. She wondered how long it would take him to come to the point. Not that she wanted him to arrive there too quickly ... Roberta's mind baulked at admitting why she had this reluctance ... it was only because – because – well, not even to herself would Roberta admit what lay beyond that "because". She told herself, tongue in cheek, that of course she was enjoying leading Muir up the garden path!

Back at Buchanan, Muir put a match to the drawing-room fire. There were gum leaves among the kindling, and they flared up immediately, crackling fiercely.

"You'll have your chimney on fire," warned Roberta.

"Not I. I have my chimneys swept twice a year. I like to pile the logs on."

"Well, don't tonight. After all, it's nearly midsummer."

"Yes, but it's turning a little chilly tonight, and I'm fond of fires."

He went across to the piano, opened it, and sat down and played a few bars; then, in a fine tenor voice began to sing "Silent Noon."

> "*Your hands lie open in the long fresh grass,*
> *The fingerpoints look through like rosy blooms;*
> *Your eyes smile peace. The pasture gleams and glooms*
> *'Neath billowing skies that scatter and amass ...*"

The song ended, he looked over his shoulder and said:

"You know what day I'm thinking of?"

She nodded. "Yes. Wednesday."

They had ridden out about half-past ten, and had flung themselves out of the saddle at noon. There had been no golden kingcups or cow-parsley such as Muir had sung about, not here in New Zealand, but there had been scented *ngaios* above their heads, and the clouds had scattered and amassed in a brassy summer sky.

He came across to where she sat on the arm of a chair.

Roberta shook herself out of her surprise and enchantment and rose quickly.

"You're full of surprises, Muir. I'd never imagined you played anything but the pipes. I didn't associate you with piano, or a tenor voice. I thought you'd be a bass . . . a growly bass at that." Her eyes danced.

Muir said slowly: "There are quite a few things you don't know about me, Roberta. Things I acquired, or achieved, after you went away. I studied for years, extramurally of course. Not only a course at Lincoln Agricultural College that your grandfather gave me time off for, but English literature, French, maths, and so on. And I took singing and piano lessons."

"Completing your education?" asked Roberta. "I rather like to think of people doing that."

Muir brushed that aside. "I had to achieve some polish," he said, "to fit into the world you live in at Heatherleigh."

Roberta looked startled, then recovered herself. How quick she was to hope there was a personal meaning behind everything he said. Of course he only meant that to become a successful landowner like Grandy, he had to somehow aspire to the same standards that obtained at Heatherleigh . . . the library full of books that were not merely ornaments, but read and read again: the objects of art, the paintings, the feeling one had in the big house of the best of the Old World linked with the best of the New.

Years ago, one wouldn't have thought of Muir as being particularly ambitious, yet he must have nursed it all the time, to have embarked on an educational programme like that. Fancy coming in night after night, tired after long days in the saddle, the drafting pens, the shearing sheds, the harvest field . . . perhaps she ought to try to understand that Muir had worked his way up from nothing, and that now the thought of further advancement was riding him.

So she said, gently: "Grandy's parents had very little when they came out here in the pioneering days, Muir. His father was the youngest son of a very impoverished family. They

87

came up from Port Chalmers with all their worldly possessions on a dray, and they lived in a sod hut at first. You've been
every bit as successful as they. Grandy had a good start, and
has achieved a wonderful estate, but he's progressed no more
than you have."

She laughed. "And my father's people were Irish peasants.
Father often talked of their whitewashed cottage, and he told
me that his own mother, as a child, shared a room with the pig,
no less . . . and that their potato pot sat in a hole in the middle of
the table, and all of them eating out of it in turn. I'm no grand
lady, Muir Buchanan, and even if I was, there is very little
social distinction in New Zealand."

She hardly knew why she said all this, save that it might
turn Muir from being too ruthless, too acquisitive . . . ?

Muir said, without expression, "There is a world of
difference, just the same, between your world and mine, if not
in ancestry, then in environment. I don't mind differences of
circumstance, I do mind the gulf between minds and learning.
And besides all that, there is something that comes between
us. Most of the time we meet on equal terms, and you are the
Roberta you used to be, impulsive and warm-hearted, then
you disappear behind a wall of reserve, and I can't reach you.
What is it?"

"I haven't a clue," said Roberta lightly. "You must imagine
it."

"I do not," said Muir. "Is it something in your life before
you came back? Something that sent you home? Did you care
for someone else?"

Someone else! That was flinging down a challenge to her to
admit she cared for him, wasn't it? He was taking a lot for
granted. The knowledge was a warning to Roberta. A
moment or so ago her feelings had betrayed her into making
excuses for him.

The dimple quivered.

"It's not likely that I'd have reached twenty-five without
having fallen in love, and out again, a few times, is it?"

"No. Few people do."

She had a swift wonder had Muir known many loves . . . he

88

was in his thirties, after all. Muir came nearer her, took her hands, looked into her eyes.

"Won't you be quite open with me, tell me what's bothering you? It isn't like you not to be open."

Anger, hot and shaking, bubbled up in Roberta. *Open*, and all Muir Buchanan concealed! She kept a rein on her temper.

She yawned, then laughed.

"Aren't we getting involved, and intense! Much ado about nothing. I thought we were going to have a pleasant evening in front of the fire, and you were going to read to me."

Muir laughed, drew a chair nearer, pulled up another for himself, and picked up a book.

"Not *Burns*?" exclaimed Roberta in mock horror.

Muir put his finger in the place, and looked at her, twinkling.

"I was going to read Browning to you," he said gently, "but I've changed my mind."

"Why?" asked Roberta promptly, adding, "I thought dour Scots never changed their minds . . . or at least admitted they did."

His eyes held hers steadily. "You have a lot to learn about dour Scots, my girl, but you will. And the reason I'm not reading you Browning is that you are in far too sceptical a mood. Browning believed in people. . . . You aren't ready to trust anyone tonight, are you, Roberta?"

She felt as chastened as she had done when Muir spanked her thirteen years ago. She dropped her eyes. She mustn't let him guess. He was too near the truth as it was. But her thoughts were bitter. *It's important to him that I should believe him, isn't it? – Because he is just playing a part, and playing it well – so well that at times I could almost believe in him.*

Muir said: "I was going to read you this too . . . Christopher Marlowe . . . know it? 'The Passionate Shepherd to His Love' . . .

> '*Come live with me and be my love,*
> *And we will all the pleasures prove*

That hills and valleys, dale and field,
And all the craggy mountains yield.'"

Roberta drew in a deep breath. This was heady stuff . . . if only it had been sincere, how sweet it would have been!

She looked up at him and her eyes were as green as a witch's.

"Yes, I know it. We learned it at school. From that Mount Helicon book of verse. Did you ever read it? No? Well, Sir Walter Raleigh, not the Elizabethan, but a professor at Oxford, wrote an answer to that. He called it 'The Nymph's Reply.' You ought to read it some time."

"Yes?" said Muir, waiting.

Her voice was mocking. "It begins:

'If all the World and Love were young,
And truth in every Shepherd's tongue
These pretty pleasures might me move
To live with thee, and be thy Love.'"

Her emphasis was light but malicious.

Muir said harshly: "I prefer Burns," picked up the bulky volume and began to read.

Roberta professed herself lazy when it came to suppertime, so Muir went out to make the coffee himself. While he was out of the room, she sat at the piano and sang just loudly enough for him to hear: "*Sigh no more, ladies, sigh no more, ladies, men were deceivers ever.*"

Roberta's voice might be singing a cynical song, but her thoughts were not with the words, though they were no less cynical. How idyllic it would have been had it been true . . . Muir cherishing a dream of some day entering her world. She realised, of course, that Muir was not only deceiving her, but himself too. What was it Daddy had once said?—That no man, however much he might associate himself with evil, ever sees himself as the villain, never analyses his motives as less than high. Muir was trying to dupe himself into believing he loved her, had, in fact, loved her a long time.

A clever line, really, and she might have fallen for it had she not overheard that conversation between Muir and Grandy. She wondered if Grandy knew the line Muir was taking . . . if they ever discussed progress. . . . He probably thought it fine, a sort of approved blueprint for love. It was as calculated as breeding stock for stud purposes, with Heatherleigh and its continuance as more important than the hearts involved.

Muir came in with biscuits and coffee. Marie's name cropped up in conversation.

"She's as beautiful as ever, isn't she?" said Roberta.

"Yes . . . like a painting. So perfect you keep looking for flaws and never finding them. The years have only added to her charm."

Roberta wasn't often as clumsy, but she blundered now.

"And as brainless as ever, I suppose," she said.

Muir rose to his feet abruptly and stood in front of the hearth, his hands clasped behind his stiff back, anger in his eyes making their tawny darkness show little red sparks.

"She is not brainless now," he said. "You forget, Roberta, that the years that have changed you have also changed and *improved* Marie. Possibly she'll never have wit, and she couldn't talk art . . . but at least she became aware of her limitations, realised charm wasn't quite enough, and deliberately set out to improve her mind. And Marie's kindness of heart makes up for a lot."

Roberta bit her lip. She had got Muir on a raw spot . . . he thought she was being intellectually snobbish, not knowing that sheer feminine jealousy, something new to Roberta, had prompted the remark. How quickly he had flown to Marie's defence!

For a moment, at least, the veneer of his pretence at courtship had been stripped aside, and he had let his true feelings show. But then, even at seventeen Marie had been dangerous, unscrupulous even, in her dealings with her own sex, upsetting several promising romances in the village, leading the lads on for the sheer delight of knowing her own power. And now Muir credited her with kindness of heart. Ye gods, weren't men blind!

She said, trying to steer the conversation back on to ordinary levels, "What does Marie do?"

Muir's voice softened. It had a curiously protective tenderness and pride.

"She gave up her job as a photographer's model to become assistant matron of a cottage orphanage in Wellington."

Surprise held Roberta quiet. *Marie!* Then she must have changed, and changed radically.

Muir continued: "She's a wonderful person, and the children adore her. It's not an easy job. The greater percentage of the children these days come not from bereaved homes but broken ones. They're much more difficult to handle. Children can accept death, as sad, but in the natural order of things. The other destroys their sense of values and their security. Marie seems to have a special knack with them."

Even when they walked home with Doss padding at their heels, through the fern-sweet cutting, over the moonlit stream with the water purling musically over its shingly bed, and through the scented garden of Heatherleigh, Muir's hand warm on her arm, Roberta felt that Marie went with them too.

Muir had felt the respect for education that every Scot knows, and Marie was keeping up with him, she supposed. Now Muir was using his acquired culture to bolster up his show of love for the heiress of Heatherleigh.

The shadow of the big house fell across them as they left the moonlit lawn. It fell across Roberta's heart too . . . for one nostalgic moment she longed for the garret studios and makeshift apartments she and her father and mother had known, where everyone shared what was going, and nobody cared what you had, or what you lacked . . . you were loved for what you were and could create.

Fortunately there was always plenty to do. Roberta found the days were very full, apportioning certain hours to her illustrating work, supervising and helping with the top floor of the big house. Grandy had tried to get her to agree to an allowance, but she was adamant.

"George gets a wage for the work he does, and a bonus at

harvest and lambing," Robert said, rather hurt that she should still be so independent, "and you work so hard, lassie."

"If I needed it, it would be different," she said. "I make a very good thing with my own work, and there is a bit of freelance illustrating too, you know, for magazines. Let's say that what I do in the house pays for my board. That will more than satisfy me."

Robert grunted, ill-pleased, yet admiring.

The old man had taken on a new lease of life. For one thing the changed conditions at the big house had filled him out again. Watching him with Meg's children, Roberta was filled with wonder. Few men of his age would have tolerated children as high-spirited as David and Josephine, but he took a rare delight in them.

At first, Meg had insisted they keep to their own quarters, but Robert was for ever breaking any rules she laid down. Not on their behaviour, though; Robert would spoil no one, and Meg was often grateful to him for supplying the man's hand in the family.

It wasn't long before Robert told Meg he would be responsible for the children's pocket money.

"But, Mr. Heatherleigh, you've done so much for them now."

He shook his head. "Only in providing a background and comfort. This is sheer pleasure."

He sent for David first, told him the amount he would allow him.

"You're to keep within that. You're going to school with all these farmers' sons around here – they have far more money than is good for them, these days, but you need to be adequately provided with pocket money. Your mother is a brick. She works like a Trojan, and does far more than I expect her to. Works happily too, which is something not all widows do.

"I want you to take over certain jobs. Some you'll like, some you won't. But you'll find that even the ones you dislike will cease to irk you, once you've mastered them. Habit, I've found, dulls the edge of beautiful things, but it also tempers our dislike of other things. There's nothing quite like coming to terms with work . . . but at your age I don't expect you to understand that.

"You'll be responsible for chopping all the kindling for the fires here, for oiling your bike, for feeding the fowls night and morning. In the May holidays you can pick potatoes for either myself, or for Buchanan. You'll get the same terms as anyone else. So much a bag. You can earn anything from twenty to thirty dollars a week then, depending on the crop and how you work. If you're wise, and fair to your mother, you'll spend a third of that on your hobbies, your Meccano and stamps, buy clothes with a third, and bank a third."

"Yes, sir," said David, sparkling-eyed, "and thank you very much." He hesitated, then added. "There isn't anything Josephine could do, is there, sir? I mean extra work like the potato picking. There doesn't seem much for girls. She said the other day she would like to earn some money to buy her own tyres for her bike for school."

Robert was pleased. He smiled at the boy from under his white eyebrows. "I'll think of something, lad," he said.

He did. Josephine was entranced. Two days later he led her out to the fowl-runs. An old one had been reconditioned and divided into two. One held a dozen seven-week-old pullets, White Leghorns, the other a couple of bantams, each sitting on a clutch of eggs.

"They're yours," said old Robert. "You'll have to look after them, mind, greens every day. Those pullets will start laying in March, and right through the winter when eggs are dear.

"The ones under the bantams will lay next spring. The estate will supply your wheat, but you'll have to buy your own mash from the time they come into the lay. You can keep a tally of all the eggs and put them in with ours when the egg truck comes. I've put aside two dozen young cockerels. You and David can take turns feeding those and fatten them to sell at Christmas. That will give you a bit of cash for presents – eh?"

He had the delight then of Josephine's warm young arms around his neck, and her soft lips against his cheek.

94

Meg's happiness grew day by day.

"It's so wonderful to have such freedom from anxiety," she said. "I used to panic when they were sick and I was at school. I couldn't stay home often. Then I would wonder how I would cope with their higher education, even with all the good bursaries available. Wondered what I'd do when they needed university, or training college, or fit them for whatever they wanted to take up."

Roberta asked: "And what about yourself, Meg? You're quite content with life here? That was the only thing I worried about . . . lest you should find it too much of a backwater. You don't get much chance of meeting people here."

Meg looked at her shrewdly.

"You mean not much chance of meeting men, don't you?"

Roberta flushed at having her thoughts read so easily.

Meg patted her hand.

"Don't worry, Roberta. It's sweet of you, but I don't feel the need of anyone here. Life is so full and so interesting. There is such a good family atmosphere in the house – a sort of clan feeling. I did miss a man's companionship, a male point of view. Do you know what I mean? A man reading the paper after dinner, digesting the world news and reading it aloud, discussing it: listening-in to Test cricket and football matches, a man's tolerance and sense of humour . . . well, your grandfather supplies all that.

"I wouldn't be foolish enough to say I'd never marry again. But one would have to be so careful not to estrange the children. My life with John was so completely satisfying, I feel I've had the best of life, anyway . . . something that even people who have celebrated their diamond wedding haven't always known. Perfect fulfilment. I admit I have my bad moments. There are times when I feel I *must* see John for just a moment, an hour, a day . . . when I feel I must write to him to tell him how Josephine has grown, how she has the same love of horses that he had, to tell him how David is doing at school. . . . Sometimes I wake up in the morning and before I struggle back to consciousness I think John is there, beside me, and I hate to wake up fully. But most of the time, I'm very happy. . . ."

Muir and her grandfather seemed to be spending a great deal of time in town, Roberta thought. But perhaps at certain times it was necessary to do all this visiting of solicitors, and accountants. Yet most of the time Muir seemed to cope with it in Grandy's study, or his own office.

It was a pity they shut George out of so much, she thought. George had a good head for figures, besides being quite expert with sheep. He was good with pigs too. Grandy had at least turned the sties over to him, and George was collecting the profits from them. But he didn't like anything to do with wheat.

He and Muir clashed badly over Muir's policy of putting a larger acreage into wheat on both Heatherleigh and Buchanan's land.

"I don't care what Muir does at Buchanan, of course," said George to Roberta moodily. "That's his pigeon, if he likes to lose money; but it goes against the grain to see him persuading the old man to employ the same policy at Heatherleigh. It could substantially impoverish the estate."

"How do you mean lose money?" asked Roberta curiously.

"Wheat's bad for the ground," said George knowledgeably. "Takes a terrific amount out of the land. Sheep enrich it. If Muir keeps on at this, Heatherleigh won't be the same place in a few years' time. Since they've got the rabbits under control they've been putting more and more down in wheat."

Roberta decided to tackle Muir about it herself, later that day. After all, Muir might justifiably feel George was only distantly connected with the estate, but she herself was Heatherleigh's granddaughter. She found him down by the sheep-pens, and tentatively introduced the subject.

"That acreage you were thinking of putting into wheat, Muir. I don't mean yours but Heatherleigh's. George thinks it would be more profitable run for sheep."

Muir's brows drew together. Now for an argument,

thought Roberta, the O'More in her warming to the fight. His reply was unexpected.

"It *would* be more profitable," he admitted.

"Then why don't you run sheep? It would be a lot less trouble, too."

Muir said, brows still drawn together, "Are we in farming just for what we get out of it?"

Roberta swept back a straying lock of her honey-gold hair, her eyes more green than brown in the strong sunlight.

"I don't get you, Muir."

"George would wring every penny he could out of Heatherleigh if it were his. Don't you realise that? A farm or an estate isn't just a way of making a living, Roberta, or of amassing wealth. It's to supply the needs of the community, the needs of the world. It's a disgrace that we here in New Zealand should have to import wheat from Australia and Canada for our own needs, with a population as small as ours. We take it from the mouths of under-privileged peoples."

Roberta felt small. She was ready to say she was sorry, but Muir swept on. The subject was evidently dear to his heart.

"I'm on the Wheat Board in Wellington, as you know. The P.M. was speaking to me very strongly on this subject a few weeks ago. I'm right behind him."

Roberta said: "The P.M.?"

Muir grinned. "Who could that mean but the Prime Minister? Don't raise your eyebrows over your grandfather's one-time shepherd hobnobbing with the P.M. After all, this is a democratic country, if ever there was one, so it doesn't mean a thing."

His tone bit. Roberta felt that after the way she had behaved at Buchanan the other night, and the brick she had dropped about Marie, Muir might well think her a little snob. She turned on her heel and left him.

His voice came with the sharpness of an order, halting her in her tracks.

"Roberta!"

She turned. He had straightened up from the railing.

"Come here." She came. "What's the matter now?"

She said wearily: "Just that you're so often smugly right, Muir Buchanan, that it's anything but endearing!"

He broke into laughter, and put out a hand to her.

"Tell me, what do I have to do, or be, to endear myself to you?"

Inwardly she said: Be like you used to be. Outwardly she said, looking up to his face appealingly: "Be nice to George."

His face hardened immediately.

"You ask me to act against my better judgment."

Roberta shrugged her shoulders helplessly.

"That reminds me: When you and George have gone into town alone, has he ever brought back any bulky packages?"

Roberta thought for a moment.

"Yes, quite often . . . why?"

"I'm not happy about it," said Muir.

Roberta said: "But what in the world has it got to do with you?"

He ignored that.

"Have you any idea what's in them?"

"If I had," said Roberta, "I'm not at all sure that I would tell you."

"Not even if it could bring disgrace upon Heatherleigh?"

"I don't know what you mean," cried Roberta. "If George brings drink back here, it's only what half the men around here do. There's no law against drinking in your own home in North Otago, is there?"

"No," said Muir. "But there is against sly-grog running."

He turned and left her.

She was in Grandy's study some time later, aimlessly looking through a pile of new magazines, when she saw Muir somewhat furtively slip into the stables, by the door that led to her quarters. Roberta opened the garden door and went quietly across to the courtyard.

She was wearing rope-soled sandals, and came quietly to the head of the stairs. She looked through into her quarters. Muir was casting about, looking for something. She decided to wait there, and confront him as he came out. This time he would be in the wrong.

Whatever Muir was looking for he wasn't finding it. But what could it be? He suddenly gave an exclamation, and went across to the west wall of the rooms where there were some high shelves, never used. He sprang up on a chair, reached up, and tugged at something far back on the shelf. He brought out a large box, dusty, and evidently heavy, and lowered himself carefully down with it. Then he ripped open the lid and drew out a bottle.

Roberta knew anger, but this time against George. She recognised the box. George had had it in the back of the car some weeks ago, there had been others since, cardboard cartons, smaller. George had no right hiding them in her quarters, especially if he was running sly-grog. She suddenly realised that Muir was going to take the box away, and now she didn't want him to see her. She had an idea Muir would handle this in his own way, and perhaps the less she was involved in it, the better.

Roberta sped down the stairs, knowing she could gain the turn in them before Muir reached the archway at the top, but she could not get to the outside door without him seeing. She darted in to the ground floor of the stables, and looked about for somewhere to hide. She saw the ladder leading to the loft and sped up it.

Just as she gained the loft she heard a step outside and knew it for George's. She felt sick. He would meet Muir at the moment when Muir would be most angry.

She heard the thump and rattle of the box going down on the stone floor, and Muir's voice, cool and determined.

"You've arrived most opportunely, George."

There was a long silence. She peeped down. George was looking at the box.

"What have you got there, Muir?" There was only polite interest in his voice.

"It won't help to pretend. In plain words it's the stuff you've been bringing out in Roberta's car. She thinks you're just bringing out a bit for yourself. Aren't you a cur, hiding it in her quarters! If the police get wind of this, Roberta could be implicated too, and she might find it very hard to clear herself.

There'll be no sly-grog running connected with Heatherleigh, George. This is the finish.

"I'd rather like to make you take your coat off and take the hiding you deserve . . . but then Heatherleigh himself would probably find out, and it would break him up a bit. He's too old for this sort of thing."

George sounded defiant. "What a fuss about very little! Just because the old man doesn't like the stuff himself, it isn't to say everyone in the district has to toe the same line."

Muir said: "It's not a question of that – you can go to Georgetown if you want it – but it's a question of breaking the law. Apart from that, and the penalties it could bring, you know how Robert Heatherleigh feels about it."

George swore. "Just because the old man's a teetotaller—"

Muir cut in. "You must be mad, George . . . you must know that the old man was no teetotaller till Ian was killed in that drunken brawl in Wellington . . . how he felt that if he'd never had it on the table, Ian might never have developed a taste for it. How dare you risk bringing all that back to Heatherleigh! It broke his heart. . . . Ian was his only surviving son, his Benjamin."

George said, in a contrite tone, "But I didn't know. Why, how should I? I've not been near Heatherleigh for years. How could I know? I knew Ian was killed, but I thought it was a street accident."

Roberta put a hand to her mouth to stop herself crying out. Only a week ago she and George had discussed the manner of Ian's death, and the tragedy of it. There had been a similar happening in the paper.

Muir looked at George. "I hope I can believe you. If there's any more of this, I'll act in a way you won't like. This time I'll overlook it. You can help me load this on to the trailer, and we'll tip it out down the dump."

George made no protest. He dared not. The two men, in silence, loaded the trailer and drove to the dump in a disused quarry on the estate.

Roberta came down from the loft considerably shaken.

CHAPTER SIX

Marie was in Oamaru, relieving for some weeks at the Home there. The day she had arrived Muir had been away from Buchanan most of the day, going down to Taeri to meet her, and then getting her installed.

They had expected him at Heatherleigh for tea, but as Muir was a generous supporter of the Orphanage, and knew the matron and staff well, they had insisted on his staying there, so he had rung from Oamaru telling them not to expect him.

Grandfather had given Roberta this message, and added: "Oh, it was good to hear Marie's voice again – she spoke to me too – she was so good when I was ill. She put fresh heart into me."

Yes, of course Marie had that effect on men; even Grandy was no exception. Roberta decided she mustn't clash with Muir so much, as she had been doing.

Marie spent all her time off at either Heatherleigh or Buchanan. Grandy asked Roberta to set aside one of the small guest rooms for her, and said to Marie: "You'll feel as if you get right off the chain, then, and when you get your two-day leave, you can come right out to stay, and get away from the atmosphere of your daily work. I should think if you have to spend the night at the orphanage, you would always be called in cases of emergency."

Marie laughed. "It does work out that way, Mr. Heatherleigh. I love it all, but a break is necessary. I'd be glad if I could do just that . . . as long as Roberta doesn't mind. Won't it make extra work for you and Meg, Roberta?"

"I shan't mind a bit," said Roberta, aware that Muir had his eye on her, and acutely conscious that she was finding it an effort to be sincere. She assumed a cordiality she was far from feeling. "You could leave some of your things here,

Marie, your sunsuits and cottons and night things. Feel free to do that, won't you?''

She earned a look of approval from Muir. So Marie spent many off-time hours at Heatherleigh, and at least Roberta thought it was better than that she spent them all at Buchanan! It was a golden November day, still and hot. Roberta hadn't found herself content with the day at all: she felt restless and fidgety. Finally, when all necessary duties had been coped with, she saddled Clancy and rode away. It would do her good, she thought, to have a mad gallop over hill and dale, letting the sweet air blow away all discontent.

At last, all cobwebs dispersed, and a sense of well-being pervading mind and body, she came to Manuka Glen, a spot on the Waianakarua that was a favourite place for picnickers on public holidays, but which today was deserted. She came to the river's edge, where the water purled musically over its rocks, and knelt beside it, cupping her hands as she drank deeply of the crystal-clear water. She wiped her hands on her handkerchief, and climbed the bank again, to a rock that was shaded from the hot sun by an overhanging *kowhai*, and a screen of *koromikos*, their veronica-like blooms glinting lilac and purple.

At first the silence seemed oppressive, then gradually she became aware of the undertones of the stillness. Faintly, and far away, a bellbird chiming above the music of the waters in the gorge, the chirping of crickets, the rustle of wings in the bushes. Roberta took an apple from her pocket, almost the last there would be now till the new season's crop, and bit into it appreciatively. She saved the core for Clancy.

Suddenly she heard another noise, above the other sounds ... voices, coming down the pass, and the unmistakable plash of paddles. She leaned forward through the leafy screen. She had never seen a craft of any kind on this river, as it was too shallow in most places, though here, where the river bluffs crowded together, it was deeper, deep enough in some places for diving.

She saw a canoe come gliding around the bend of the river, and be lost to sight the next moment beneath dark, overhanging cliffs. Roberta knew enchantment. It was idyllic.... So might some Maori of other days have come, piloting his graceful craft, ferrying his pretty *wahine* down to the sea.

But it wasn't a Maori and his *wahine* ... it was a tall, bronzed man, like a Red Indian ... and a Norse princess ... Marie, dipping her fingers in the cool water as they moved slowly along, Muir paddling.

Instinctively Roberta shrank back into the bushes. They would soon be past. The canoe came into water too shallow and became marooned. Muir laughed.

"Oh, well, we might as well have afternoon tea here as anywhere."

Marie said lazily: "Not trying to cover up your lack of skill as a navigator, are you, Muir? Because you needn't, I assure you. It's rather refreshing to find you not the master of every situation for a change."

Roberta had the odd conviction that for once she shared a fellow feeling with Marie. He was so sure of himself.

Muir chuckled, no whit perturbed.

"No one would bring a canoe down this temperamental river without getting stranded half a dozen times. Marie ... stop being purely a decoration to my canoe, and pass over the flask and sandwiches, will you?"

The fact that Roberta could have done with a cup of tea herself did nothing to lessen her discomfort. Not having called out right away, she was now forced into being an eavesdropper.

Marie said: "I can't help thinking you had an ulterior motive in getting aground just here.... You were trying to change the subject, weren't you?"

Roberta saw Muir measure glances with Marie.

"Yes," he admitted. "I thought you were getting far too intense, my dear. A great pity on a glorious afternoon like this, meant for nothing more pleasant than small talk."

He leaned forward and patted her knee.

"It may all come out right yet. I've got rather a faith in happy endings," he said.

"Have you?" asked Marie, and her tone was bitter. "But then it's easier for you to hold that belief ... you know what you want and how to get it." She dropped the subject abruptly. "I think I made this tea too weak, but you'll have to make the best of it."

Muir surveyed the milky-looking fluid grimly.

"I'll teach you to make a decent cup of tea yet, my lass."

Marie said suddenly: "I've just thought: How on earth do we get back to Buchanan? We can't paddle this thing upstream, can we?"

Roberta caught the flash of white in Muir's tanned face as he smiled.

"I've been waiting for you to ask that ever since we left home. When we get around Pigeon Bluff, we disembark and, carrying the canoe, go around the gullies home. It's only about two and a half miles."

Marie gazed at him, speechless.

He laughed again. "I know you don't like walking, you never did. You really ought to have been born in another generation, Marie, and always have gone abroad in your carriage and pair."

His tone was indulgent. Muir liked Marie's femininity.

Roberta thought of the walks she and Muir had taken together, going through the pass, with its rough boulders, and right up to the top of Government Hill; mushrooming expeditions, when they must have walked miles; roaming over hill and dale right to the sea, miles away ... she had been employing the wrong technique; she must be more feminine, less robust. She found it quite easy, and, after all, she had a better innings than Marie, who was tied to the routine of the orphanage. It was wonderful how Marie enjoyed the work, for there was no forty-hour week about it, or even a compensating salary. But of course Marie had a small private income – not enough to attract Muir, who played for high stakes, reflected Roberta unhappily, but enough to keep Marie in clothes.

Roberta and Muir continued to spend most of their spare time together, several times going south to Dunedin to plays and operas, and once to the ballet. Roberta hadn't expected to be asked to that last . . . one just didn't associate Muir with a liking for ballet. The spoken word, yes, for that would appeal to most Scotsmen, as would music, but not drama interpreted in rhythm, and movement. Roberta decided she might still have a lot to learn about Muir.

One evening the following week Muir told Roberta he was taking a quick trip to Australia the next day. They were walking in the garden at Heatherleigh.

Roberta was amazed. Shearing had just finished. They had done it in record time, for not a drop of rain had dampened the fleeces, and all the shearers they needed had turned up. Muir had recorded this fact in what he called Buchanan's log book, something he thought might be of interest to future generations. But the haymaking would be early this year, and with Christmas looming near she would have thought it would have been far too busy for Muir to have gone away.

"Are you after stud sheep?"

"Well, it's to do with stud. Selling them, actually. I'm going over to Tasmania from Australia too. But we don't want George to know. He can think I'm just in Wellington."

"Why not?"

"Well, he was running sly-grog. I think he's realised he'd better leave it alone, but I'm frightened he might play up if he thinks I'm out of the country. Your grandfather would be so upset if he knew, and if he got into a rage at his age, anything could happen.

"If George shows any signs of cutting up rough in any way, go for Andy. He's a good sort in time of trouble. I'll tip him off. Meanwhile, don't worry. Go ahead with the Christmas preparations. I won't be long. It's only two hours to Sydney, you know. Bit different from the time it took four days to cross the pond, and the ships were infrequent too. I'll garage the car in Christchurch and be back on Monday morning."

Muir looked down at Roberta. She was wearing something white, finely pleated, and filmy. Her eyes were bright in the moonlight.

"Would you like me to bring you something back from Sydney, Roberta?"

"No, I don't think so, Muir, thank you . . . oh, yes, there is something. I want some little Chinese bowls for soup and rice. I'll tell you where to get them. I'll run in and get you some money."

Muir caught her by the arm.

"I asked you what I could bring you. Don't spoil my pleasure by paying for them yourself." His smile was tender. What was there about this man? she wondered. Had he a nature that warred constantly against itself? He could be so gentle, so considerate, like the old Muir, then it was suddenly overlaid by the ruthlessness of the land-grabber.

Muir drew her deeper into the shadows. They were in the orchard now, and there was the tumbledown wall where they had lingered that night. They were crushing the self-sown wallflowers with their feet, and the wholesome perfume came up to them. Muir bent, picked her up, and swung her over the wall.

He drew her beneath the shadows of the big pear. Roberta despised herself for the weakness that always came over her at his nearness. She could never marshal her doubts and distrust when his arms were around her. He tilted her chin up with one finger.

She said, uncertainly, the words surprised out of her: "You don't hear of many aircraft accidents over the Tasman, these days, do you?"

He laughed. "You don't hear of any, my foolish Roberta."

For all his laughter, she could see he liked her foolishness, her little fears for him. A warning bell in her mind told her it was only because it made him more sure of

Heatherleigh. She didn't know what had made her say it. It shouldn't matter to her, but it did, it did.

The moon came out from behind a cloud, illumining Muir's face, lighting up the dark eyes under the craggy brows. This could be a wonderful moment, thought Roberta, if only she had not heard him plotting with Grandfather. . . . The hard lips came down on hers, blotting out all unwelcome thoughts. Suddenly all her defences were down. As he released her, she drew near him again, ran her hands up his jacket to the lapels, and kissed him back. At that moment they heard Meg calling Roberta from the house.

"Toll call from Auckland," she added, as they answered her.

Roberta knew regret and relief oddly mingled . . . just as well the toll call had come. Moments like these threatened to weaken her resolve, to cloud the fact that this was pretence on Muir's part, and only made him feel more sure of one day sharing her inheritance.

Yes, he was getting more sure of her, she thought, for as she sped towards the house, and the toll call from Supplefits, she heard him take the road to Buchanan whistling *"A hundred pipers and a' and a'."*

CHAPTER SEVEN

ROBERTA took seriously the advice about keeping George out of mischief. The hot weather was taking toll of Grandy's newly-regained air of health, and she did not want him upset. Also, a less worthy reason, it would be very satisfying to make Muir Buchanan admit, if only to himself, that things could go on quite smoothly without him.

She hoped that the weather stayed as it was, so that the haymaking would proceed at a speed that Muir would be forced to comment on favourably, and that George would work so hard that Grandy would have to admit he had, however ungrudgingly. George, to her eyes, appeared chastened. She could see he was a little uneasy, not sure if Muir might have told her of his defection or not, and had probably come to the conclusion that he would be foolish to jeopardise the chances he had at Heatherleigh.

Roberta had a longing to tie up all the ends of the stories at Heatherleigh. She wanted to see Grandfather happy, tranquil in his old age, worrying no more about how Heatherleigh would be carried on when he was concerned with the things of this world no longer; to see George settle down, to be satisfied with the good wage Grandy paid him till such time as he could be trusted with the management. In fact, she wanted George to be as he had been once.

And Muir? She would like Muir to have a fine scorn of consequence, to be to Heatherleigh what he used to be, working for the sake of working, kind because he could not help being kind. Perhaps there were other things she should wish for Muir too . . . but if Marie had any place in them – no. She wasn't big enough for that. She wanted any dreams he had to enfold Roberta O'More, loving her for herself alone.

The days were brilliant, with hard blue skies and never a cloud. Andy and McGregor decided to start bringing the hay in. They used balers and the work proceeded with incredible speed.

Meg and Roberta worked hard, baking and brewing, and once on a glorious day when the children had an unexpected holiday from school, they all helped build a small stack.

That was a piece of sheer sentiment on Grandy's part. Roberta had said wistfully, looking at the huge hay shelters, built in on two sides against the weather, and sturdily roofed. "Not half as romantic as haystacks, are they? Do you remember, George, what fun we had in the one by the creek? We used to get so wet, building dams and paddling around, then we would climb up there and dry off in the sun."

Grandy had given orders next day for a stack to be built in the same place, for Henk and Josephine and David. It was idyllic, wielding the forks, urging old Dobbin, the Clydesdale, to further effort. (They were sure, by his reluctance, that he thoroughly approved of the more modern methods.) The fragrance of the new-mown hay was everywhere, and the drift of perfume came from a nearby paddock of red clover.

George was in a teasing mood, romping with the children, flirting outrageously with Meg and Roberta, both of them looking a mixture of ancient and modern in slacks, tartan shirts, and two enormous sunbonnets they had unearthed.

"You ought to be in lilac prints," said George, "with long full skirts kilted up over umpteen petticoats."

Why couldn't George always be like this? thought Roberta. One wouldn't regret the changing years so much then. That night, over a late dinner, the sense of family and harmony was noticeable, and later the four of them played cards till their yawns drove them to an early supper.

George offered to lock up, but that was one job old Robert would yield to no one. Roberta thought that was a pity, as it made George seem like an irresponsible youngster. Meg said goodnight and went off to her own quarters.

George said: "It's been a big day, so come on. Andy thinks we ought to start haying at Buchanan tomorrow."

He held out his hand to Roberta. Hand in hand they climbed the stairs, and paused at her door. The moonlight shafted through the uncurtained casement of a window at the end of the hall. The lines of George's face were softened. In a light like this Roberta could recall the young George without effort, something she could never do by daylight. In daytime she was somehow aware that George had lived hardily. A nostalgic tenderness flashed upon her. The young boy had been so idealistic, so daring, so quixotic. What changes there must have been in his life, to harden him, to coarsen the fineness that had been in him. George needed someone to help him, to love and to understand him. A woman behind him.

So when George bent to her, she lifted her face and kissed him.

They heard Grandy's step on the landing. He said gruffly, "Now, come on, youngsters, it'll be another big day tomorrow."

They both laughed, feeling like youngsters indeed, caught out rifling the larder, and parted. But Roberta's smile was wry. Grandy certainly watched over Muir's interests.

On Sunday night she knew a traitorous gladness that Muir was coming home. He would be leaving Sydney at three in the morning – New Zealand time. It would be one o'clock in Sydney, and his plane would touch down at Harewood by eight or thereabouts, depending on the wind, following or otherwise. On Monday morning she went over and did out the rooms at Buchanan, set fresh flowers in the vases, and filled the tins in the larder. Some impulse drove her to look in the drawer of the bedside table. The miniature was no longer there.

She looked thoughtfully at the space it had occupied. Then she told herself sternly that she need not think Muir had taken it across the Tasman with him. . . . It would only mean he had put it in a safe place till the house was occupied again.

He would have an idea that it was valuable, since Grandy must have taken it out of the Heatherleigh safe to give to him, so all it would mean was that Muir had put it in his own safe.

She had a sudden thought, and went into the empty bedroom at the front of the house. It smelt stale, so she opened the windows while she was there. There was dust lying thickly across the floor, as well there might be in this hot, nor'west weather with the dry wind blowing limestone dust in every crack and crevice. She could see her own footsteps right across it.

Another set too, much larger ones, leading from the door, across to the inner nursery door. She opened it. The footsteps went across to the press where Marie's photograph had lain. She went across, pulled open the drawer. It wasn't quite empty; the frame still lay there, and the shattered glass, but the photo had gone. Easy to imagine why . . . a photograph minus frame was easier to pack!

Roberta wished she hadn't come up to find out. She felt a distaste for her own action . . . and if she could fit these happenings together as easily as a jigsaw, no doubt other folk could too. She didn't want Muir to know she had been prying. She shut the window, got a broom, and swept the floor.

Grandy seemed to think Muir would be late back.

"We'll have dinner late," he said to Roberta privately. "Will you tell Meg? Buchanan is doing some business for me in Christchurch. George thinks Muir is coming over on the ferry from Wellington this morning. It would be the *Hinemoa*, so remember. I think we were wise not to let George know, in case he slacked."

"And he didn't, did he?" said Roberta eagerly, seizing the opportunity of boosting George. "He worked like a Trojan."

"He did," said Grandfather. "He can work when he likes, but he's so unstable and temperamental. I had a talk with George a few days ago – that's why he's pepped up. After all, George would sooner please me than displease me. He doesn't want to be cut out of my will." His tone was dry.

Roberta went white. It sounded so mercenary.

She said, with reluctance: "I have to admit that that's

111

probably true enough. I'm disappointed George has turned out like this, too, but sometimes when I think of the youngster he used to be, I think there may be reasons for it . . . that life may have dealt him some hard blows."

She looked appealingly at her grandfather.

He shook his head, not angrily, not impatiently, but sorrowfully.

"George was here a long time before you came back, lassie, and we found out a lot about him we didn't like. Don't think I'm being hard. I tried to find excuses for him at first, in fact far too many . . . you see, I had my heart set on a Heatherleigh inheriting Heatherleigh."

He paused, his eyes distant.

"But now there'll be no one of my name to come." He turned and looked at her. "Your children will inherit it, Roberta, but they won't be Heatherleighs."

She spoke coolly, deliberately, hoping to provoke him to coming out into the open.

"You never know . . . I might marry someone who would be willing to change his name by deed poll."

Robert Heatherleigh looked at her.

"It's a big thing to expect a man to give up his own birthright. I hope you'll marry a man above that sort of bargaining. But you might manage it." He chuckled. "After all, you're a fascinating piece."

Roberta didn't smile back. *Above that sort of bargaining!* How could Grandy be so insincere? She turned to go out of the room.

Her grandfather said: "Don't get too involved with George, will you? He isn't the sort to play around with."

Which was precisely why Roberta went fishing with George soon after lunch.

It was delightful at the Pool of Darkness. Stiflingly hot in the full sun, here the heat was tempered with tree shade. There was a great outcropping of rock above the glade, overhanging in a ridge.

Muir had once said there would probably be lime under

112

the ridge, valuable if brought out, but Robert Heatherleigh had no wish to see a white gash cut into the hillside he loved and a road cut through. This place was in the middle of the estate.

A huge *totara* tree crowned the knoll, and beneath it was what the children called the Balancing Rock, since they had read some old Zane Grey books in Grandy's library. It did look as if it would pivot round, but there were plenty of smaller rocks at its base to support it, and it was embedded in earth too.

The children had made Roberta quite uneasy, she had laughingly told them, the last time they had picnicked here.

Perhaps that was why it attracted her attention so much this afternoon? She looked around at the rock more than once.

"What's the matter?" asked George.

"I don't know, but just the last few moments I've had the oddest sensation. I wondered, if we had an earthquake, would that rock come down?"

"We don't get many earthquakes," said George lazily.

"No, that's true," said Roberta. "But I can't help it this afternoon. I've got a strange feeling . . . almost as if we were being watched."

George nodded. "I've had that before, in lonely places."

They had finished fishing, and evidence of their skill, or their luck, lay gleaming pink and silver beside them on the grass. A hamper lay there too. Roberta was packing the cups away, George leaning back against a willow, smoking. He tossed his cigarette butt away, carefully standing on it, sat down, and reached for Roberta's hand.

She smiled at him. "This has been like old times, George."

George smiled down on her. "I've been a fool, Roberta. I've realised that this week. But here, today, I've felt that this is life at its best. I've been very unsettled till now."

Roberta's look was radiant. "George, I'm so glad."

"I've been a slacker of late years, Roberta . . . I'll admit that. There are things in my life that I regret. But there hasn't

113

been anyone to care, so it didn't seem to matter. Now it does."

George moved nearer.

"You know what I mean. If I had someone like you to keep me on the straight and narrow, it wouldn't be hard. Roberta, you could care, couldn't you? I find you bewitching." He pulled her to him.

Roberta sprang to her feet, laughing.

"Let's not be too serious," she said.

George said, impatiently: "You haven't got any stupid bug in your head about cousins not marrying, have you? Because the relationship is too distant to matter, you know."

"I know that," said Roberta, and would have said more, but George kissed her, stifling her protests, if indeed they had been protests that trembled on her lips.

She could have been keeping the situation light, or she could have been being deliberately provocative.

She bent down and picked up a salmon by its tail, waved it gaily in the air.

"George, this isn't the time or the place. I'm covered with fish scales, and horribly sunburnt. Try me by moonlight some time. Meg will be pleased with us. Yours must be a fourteen-pounder, and mine not much less. Come on, George. I promised Meg I'd set the table, and do the flowers for her."

Back home again, Roberta changed, did the table and the flowers, then had a bath and changed again by the time Muir came back to Heatherleigh.

She wore black, a long filmy dress, the honey-gold hair pale above it, Muir's *paua* shell necklace gleaming above it with all the charm of the opalescent sea from which it had come.

She met Muir's eyes once across the table and felt a traitorous gladness that he was home again. She dropped her eyes as she felt the hot colour in her cheeks.

George was busy talking to Heatherleigh, but Meg noticed the blush and was glad. She wanted Roberta to marry Muir. It was much later before Muir got the chance to

114

say to Roberta: "I've got your bowls with me. They're in the study. I'll go in there later, and perhaps you could slip in after me, unobserved."

Roberta nodded. George, as an Australian, would be bound to recognise the bowls from Sydney's Chinatown. Half an hour later Muir said to Heatherleigh: "I'll just go into your study and look over those records from the Waiareka Sale if I may, sir."

The old man nodded from his seat near the great fireplace.

"Aye . . . they're not on the desk – I think I left them on top of the big filing cabinet."

Roberta said casually a few moments later that she must go over to get some adverts she had ready for the morning's rural mail clearance. She did go to get them, from her studio, but they took her only a few moments to collect together, then she came running through the scented darkness to the door that gave from the study to the rose garden. Her light evening sandals made no sound as she came up the steps.

As her hand closed over the knob she heard voices. She paused, disappointed. It was Grandfather. He must have wanted to see Muir. She decided to wait, as he might not be long.

Grandfather's voice came clearly to her.

"She's inclined to let her sympathies run away with her, and George is playing up to it." He snorted. "He even came to church with us yesterday. She's so like Ishbel . . . my wife was so impulsive and warm-hearted. I hope the lassie doesn't have any ideas about reforming him. They bade each other a very tender goodnight the other night."

There was a pause. Then when Muir spoke his voice was grim.

"Yes. I didn't go straight over home this afternoon. When Meg said they'd taken their bathing suits with them, I borrowed your hack and followed them up."

Roberta controlled a gasp of fury and surprise. So he had followed them! She clenched her fists.

Muir continued: "You know how I feel about bathing at the Pool of Darkness. It's still treacherous with snags."

115

Roberta unclenched her fists. Oh, well, it could be solicitude.

The next moment she was angry again.

"I stayed to watch them. Quite a touching scene."

Her cheeks burned at that note in Muir's voice.

"George was asking her to marry him. She said neither yes nor no. I think she was just leading him on for the sheer fun of it."

Oh, no, Muir, it's you I'm leading on, but not for fun.

The old man grunted.

"I'll back you," he said. "George is no man for a woman to ride the water with. It would break my heart for her to marry George. I was very worried while you were away, but I dared not say too much. She's not as headstrong as Hester, yet all through these years I've wished I'd not been so opposed to *her* marriage with Stephen O'More. It only strengthened the attraction he had for her, and, in any case — I was wrong there. I thought he might have been as fickle and unstable in his affections as he was in living here, there, and everywhere, but he was faithful, and he made Hester happy . . . but I lost my daughter."

That could have meant a lot to Roberta, knowing that Grandy regretted his opposition to her parents' marriage, but all that had gone before had frozen her thoughts.

Her hands were icy. Maybe Mother and Father had been wiser, after all, not to love the land, but to make the whole world their home. You could love one spot too much, and to keep it in the hands you wanted it kept in you were prepared to be ruthless and calculating.

She hoped that when she was old she would feel that her stewardship of her possessions ended then. Something read years ago leapt to her mind . . . "and all you can take in your cold dead hand is what you have given away." But some people wanted to reach out beyond the grave and impose their will on future generations.

Muir said: "Roberta is coming to the study to meet me. She commissioned me to buy her something in Sydney, so I thought it best to see her here to give it to her."

Robert chuckled.

"That wouldn't be your only reason for wanting to see her alone!"

Roberta didn't hear Muir's reply. She heard the opening and the closing of the study door into the hall.

It was just as well she had overheard the conversation, for the knowledge of it would armour her against believing in Muir. When she was with him it was hard to go on thinking he was capable of scheming. She had perceived in herself of late a tendency to minimise it, had even thought tenderly at times how wonderful it would be to please Grandy, to give him the desire of his heart. She must steel herself against this wishful thinking.

She thought of the time when she had so despised other girls for being taken in by fascinating scoundrels. Wondered at their lack of judgment, and wondered how mere physical attraction could so blind them to true worth of character. But hadn't she been guilty of the same thing? Knowing with her mind that Muir was deceiving her, yet when she was with him surrendering her reason to her feelings. That must be it.

This proved it beyond shadow of doubting. So he'd been uneasy about her being with George! Oh, if only she had known Muir had been listening on the slope above the pool, she would have seen to it that he would have been even more uneasy.

She put up her hand and tapped lightly on the door. Muir had the door open for her in a moment, and had swept her into the lighted study, and, closing the door, brought her into his arms.

His mouth came down on hers, seeking response and finding it. In spite of herself, Roberta thrilled to his touch. At last he lifted his mouth from hers, but kept her close, still in the circle of his arms, his eyes looking down into hers.

"I kept wondering all the way across the Tasman, and back, if I'd only dreamed you kissed me before I left. . . . What's the matter? Are your eyes dazzled after being out in the dark?"

Roberta passed her hand over her eyes and nodded. It was as good an excuse as any for the fact that she couldn't hold his gaze and hide that her heart was flooded with pain.

She turned her face against his jacket, and stood there against him till she could subdue her emotions.

Then she said: "I don't think we should spend too long in here. I said I was collecting my mail from the studio. Where are the bowls?"

Muir released her.

"Here they are. I managed to get spoons to match."

They were lovely, bright, and oriental-looking. Roberta had a wry thought. She wondered if, when Muir had purchased them, he had thought that they might be packed in a hope chest, and that some day they might grace his table at Buchanan.

Her eyes blurred as she looked at the bowls, suddenly nostalgic for a meal in Sydney's Chinatown, somewhere light and bright, with all the noise of a big city about her, released from the responsibilities of the land and the legacies of the future.

"I found Sydney a pulsing place," said Muir. "So flamboyant and beautiful, full of contradictions ... narrow streets and wide parks, and tall buildings after the American style sitting cheek by jowl with offices that were squat and English. A sense of history behind it ... not always a happy history, but a courageous one ... and a sense that it's growing too fast.

"The mounted police controlling the traffic at noon took me back to the cities of Britain, of course, and everywhere you turned there was a glimpse of the blue sea, and the enchanting skyline of masts and derricks." His eyes twinkled. "And then, of course, there was THE BRIDGE!"

Roberta chuckled with him, finding the lighter moments easier to bear, picked up her bowls, re-wrapped them, and put them in the bookcase.

"I'll get them from here tomorrow, and take them up to the studio." She turned to go. "I must be away," she said, forestalling any more embraces, and was gone on the words.

Muir was back in the hall when she came in again, teasing Meg over something.

If, for the next few days, Roberta grieved, no one would have known it. She was gay, laughing, and constantly singing if she thought anyone was within hearing, and if Muir or Marie were about, gayer than ever.

Marie was extremely busy. Things always piled up at the Homes just before Christmas, she said, checking up on all the places that were offering to take the children for the holidays, and trying desperately hard to get them all placed where they would be happy and find kindred interests.

The children varied so, according to the backgrounds from which they had come. Some loved the city life, some the country, others the sea. Heatherleigh was to take three, all of one family, something old Robert hadn't been able to do for many years. It warmed his heart to throw open his doors again. Muir was helping Marie plan her part of the Orphanage treat, so they were spending many hours together.

The haymaking proceeded. Several times big thundery clouds rolled up and threatened to spoil the last of it, but each time they rolled right back above the mountains, and circled around to South Canterbury, where they had had plenty of rain and where the pastures were green and lush still.

"We'll expect rain when the clouds touch down on the foothills and curl up in shapes like whisky bottles," said Muir, and in answer to Roberta's look of inquiry said: "In the old days, an old swagger used to call in, and he always said: 'You get rain in North Otago when there are whusky bottles on the foothills.' He's right too."

There would be little leisure time at Heatherleigh till Christmas and New Year were over.

"It's worse just now," said Muir. "With the season dry like this, the grass seed will be ready to harvest before the holiday period is over. There's no doubt about it, farming is much less complicated at home. Christmas is a delightful period, making a welcome and leisurely break in mid-winter."

"I often think that," said Meg. "I envy them the summer holidays in July and August. When we were on our Taranaki farm, it often happened that John couldn't get away at all in the January when the children were home. I used to take them away for a fortnight, but I missed John horribly, and felt very guilty about leaving him at so busy a time. Then when I got home, I always found the fruit had ripened and the birds had most of it. I've always felt the southern hemisphere is badly planned to have Christmas, summer holidays, and the jam-making season and harvest all lumped together."

Roberta wasn't as fond of her own company as she once had been. When you were alone all sorts of regrets came to poison the tranquillity of solitude.

Even sitting in the beautiful Presbyterian church at Heatherleigh she was conscious of a sense of desolation, a loss of belief in the people she loved most.

Robert had built St. Ninian's. He wanted something more durable than Oamaru stone, which chipped badly, but had a deep-rooted belief that one ought to build in the materials that belonged to the district. He had had experts down, and happily they had found a more rock-like stone on the estate itself.

The church was roofed with the bright tiles that suited the North Otago countryside so well, and the furnishings were carried out in some of the most beautiful of the native woods.

There were individual carvings on every pew, and on font and lectern, pulpit and organ, carvings of native birds and trees. There were *tuis*, fantails, bellbirds, *pukekes*, the *takahe*, that when St. Ninian's was built had been supposedly extinct, until a small colony of them had been found in the fiordland near Te Anau. There were *kowhais, clematis, rata, pohutakawa*.

The Reverend Donald Murray was universally beloved, and not only by his own flock; he was a man's man, short and stocky, with powerful shoulders, a man who visited the men of his parish in their own fields.

He was always there as a spare man at harvesting time, provided his own work would not suffer, working on the grain harvesters, lending a hand with the shearing, if wet weather threatened.

When he had been approached about coming to St. Ninian's, he had come to preach, as was the custom, and looked the parish over, then told the selection committee he had decided not to accept their call. They had asked why. He had been direct.

"I don't want to hurt anyone's feelings. I love the church. Interior beauty is what some of our Presbyterian churches lack, particularly our country ones. They're too bare and plain. I've always enjoyed helping in the ones I served, to create a richer atmosphere of worship . . . something of the beauty of holiness. So it would mean a lot to me to be minister of a place like this. But — and it's a big 'but' — it savours too much of a one-man show. I believe I'd prefer a plainer, less lovely building because I might find more freedom in it. I don't doubt that your Robert Heatherleigh is a great benefactor, but he could easily be a dictator too."

Robert had heard of this, chuckled, and asked Donald Murray to come to see him.

"You sound a man after my own heart," he said. "So you think you might be hamstrung by the fact that Heatherleigh money has paid for the kirk?"

"Exactly," said Donald Murray, crisply, with no apologies in word or tone.

"You're the man we need," said Robert. "I shan't say want. We've had some good men here, but the last man was far too careful not to offend me. I didn't blame him — only I found it hard to get to grips with the situation, and it took him three years or more to realise that the church was entirely his province, and the estate was mine."

So Donald Murray came to the charge, and had never regretted it, and his friendship with Robert Heatherleigh was good to behold.

Now Roberta O'More, the last of the family, sat in a pew between her grandfather and Muir Buchanan, with Meg and the children in the same row, and wondered if she had been wise to return to Heatherleigh. Not that there was any question of her leaving. She loved her grandfather too dearly for that, and him she could forgive ... but not Muir Buchanan.

The hay was finished, and two days after it was all in they had a most refreshing rain, something that would plump out the orchard fruit, and revive the drooping garden flowers as no amount of watering with the hose could do. It was a warm rain, and didn't last long enough to split the cherries.

Everyone took time off for shopping for Christmas presents in Oamaru, and Meg and Roberta even went as far afield as Dunedin for one of their expeditions. It should have been a happy time, for it had all the trappings to make it so.

Grandfather had spared no pains to make it a memorable Christmas for the youngsters. Roberta always missed, at this season, when she was in the southern hemisphere, the traditional touches of the English and Continental Christmases she had known ... the robins bright against the snow, the holly berries lighting up the dim corners of age-old churches, the mistletoe and the ivy, the wreathed hoops in the windows, the lanterns bobbing down a village street.

Muir helped them with the decorations, bringing in the prickly holly, and suggesting to Roberta that she tuck in scarlet geraniums to provide the right touch of brightness. He brought masses of native evergreens, and spruce, pine, and larch, and plenty of evergreens, and by the time they had decorated the huge tree that Grandy provided for the children on the estate, and put the finish to the two great cakes Meg had made so professionally, Roberta knew that Christmas could be just as lovely here in Maoriland ... if only things had been as they had been once.

They had the usual Colonial Christmas dinner ... homegrown lamb, sweet and succulent, new potatoes, green peas, mint sauce, and a plum pudding to which they would have done greater justice on a colder day.

Later in the afternoon, when all was safely digested, they

went bathing up at Yellowstone Ford, Roberta and Meg returning earlier than the others to put the finishing touches to the party tea set out under one of the big cedars.

New Year's Eve was the occasion of the estate ball, held in the great hall with its lovely parquet floor. Roberta had gone to a great deal of trouble over the choice of a new gown, finally getting one in Auckland. If this didn't bring Muir to the proposing point, she would be surprised.

She was suddenly weary of it all. When she had paid Muir out in his own coin, she would recover from her heartache, and it would cease to matter any more.

Muir would be early at the ball, for he was to be the piper for the occasion. Roberta was glad. She and her grandfather would be early, too, to receive the guests. A staircase gave such an impressive entrance, especially one like the Heatherleigh stair.

She came around the curve of the great *kauri* staircase, tiny on her grandfather's arm, but every inch the mistress of Heatherleigh.

Folds of yellow gauze billowed out over layers of palest green underslips, and a diaphanous cloud of gold swathed her creamy shoulders and was caught at the breast, fichu fashion, with a tiny silken spray of mimosa. Here and there the skirt was caught with more tiny sprays, and against the pale gold of her hair was another, but this time in gold filigree, studded with amber – Grandy's New Year gift to her.

She paused, one hand on the newel rail, and looked down. Muir was there, but not alone. Marie was with him.

Grandfather paused too, well pleased with this moment for the two people he loved best in the world. For him, Marie was only a vague extra on the stage.

But for Roberta, Marie dominated the scene. She was in an oyster-coloured satin dress, swathed with sophisticated cunning. Suddenly Roberta felt like a girlish debutante. Marie had a heavy, barbaric-looking gold necklace close about her beautiful throat, and bracelets to match on her wrists. Yes, a Norse goddess. . . .

Before long they were swept into the crowds and excitement of the ball. In the main the dances were the old-fashioned ones such as Grandy loved, with here and there some of the new to satisfy the young fry from college or university who were home on the estate or in the village for the holidays.

There were toddlers and babies parked in all the bedrooms, and the guests from the Heatherleigh Arms had turned out in full force, lending a little sophistication to the occasion.

George danced several times with Roberta, and she found him a perfect partner. The dance was half over before Muir came to her, but then he'd been busy piping for most of the time, and when he hadn't been Roberta had noticed how attentive he had been to the few wallflowers, mostly shy young girls, dancing with them himself, and unobtrusively bringing up younger partners for them.

Their dance was a waltz. Meg was at the piano, and Henk's uncle was playing the piano accordion. Roberta hadn't expected Muir to be so expert a dancer, so light on his feet, or able to suit his step so well to hers in spite of the difference in their heights.

"This compensates me for my duty dances," he said to the top of her head. Roberta nodded. She didn't want to talk, for this was one of the moments when the knowledge of the duplicity that was in Muir was almost beyond bearing.

Marie hadn't lacked partners all night. From Muir's arms Roberta looked across at her.

"Isn't Marie exquisite?" she said. "I should imagine she turns every head in the street."

Muir nodded, rather absently, then said: "Yes ... she reminds me of something once said of Mary, Queen of Scots. A man who had seen her was asked: 'Is she really so beautiful?' and he replied: 'I don't know, but some women walk in a glory!' "

Roberta turned her cheek against his shoulder so he should not see her face. So ... for Muir Buchanan, Marie Sylvester walked in a glory.

124

Presently she found the grace to say: "You were right about her . . . there *is* more to her than there used to be. Or did I perhaps carry away the wrong idea of her as a child? I find my early impressions aren't a bit reliable –" (there was a hint of bitterness here) "– but when she was sixteen, or was it seventeen? – she was such a – such a —"

Muir laughed. "Such an arrant little flirt," he finished for her. His voice was indulgent. Roberta thought impatiently what fools men were. 'An arrant little flirt' – Why, even at that age Marie had made more mischief in the village than the rest of the girls put together. She had been quite unscrupulous, breaking up several promising matches, merely for the satisfaction of knowing her own power, not because she had cared a rap about any of the local lads. Roberta supposed men were always indulgent where a pretty girl was concerned.

She could still remember Muir saying: "I spanked George and Roberta yesterday. . . . A spanking would be good for you too, Marie!"

Marie had turned the full battery of her eyes upon Muir, looking wise beyond her years, and had said: "Ah, caveman tactics."

But Muir was still talking of present-day Marie.

"She's not the empty little fool she used to be. She learned her lessons slowly. She's grown in spirit and in mind now."

That was probably true enough. No woman would take on caring for orphans unless she had deeps within her.

Muir seemed to realise he was hardly furthering his cause by talking solely of Marie, for now he bent to the top of Roberta's head and said:

"Keep the midnight waltz for me?" It was more of an order than a request. "It's the custom here to switch off the lights just before the clock strikes . . . most of the girls get kissed, I imagine, then the lights come on as the last stroke sounds. Everyone rushes in with New Year wishes, and the first-foot comes in. I'm first-foot this year. I'm dark enough, you see, and not flat-footed. I go out through the study and the garden door, and in through the front entrance."

As the lights went out in the midnight waltz, they were right beside the study door. Muir opened it noiselessly and drew Roberta in with him.

"I was going to stay," she protested.

He laughed confidently.

"I'm not wishing you a Happy New Year in the midst of a crowd like that."

He held her lightly as he had done in the dance, then bent to her and said: "Whenever I see the sunlight shining through the mimosa at the Mill Weir I'll think of you in this gown." His fingers touched the gauzy folds briefly. "Or do you, as a dinkum Aussie, call it wattle?"

Roberta thought: He's retrieving his error in talking so much of Marie. . . .

Aloud she said: "I call it mimosa too . . . after living so long in the South of France."

Just then the big clock in the hall finished its beautiful chiming, and began to strike.

Muir stooped his head.

"Last year was a magic one, Roberta, because it brought you back. This year . . ." he paused, laid his cheek against hers . . . "well . . . this doesn't give me much time. I'll leave it for now, and just wish you the old, old wish . . . Happy New Year." His lips brushed hers, and then he released her and was gone across the room to the garden door.

Roberta put a hand to her mouth as she fumbled for the handle of the inside door. She mustn't weep . . . Grandy loved New Year, and she must find him, he would be looking for her.

Back in the lighted hall amidst the laughter and merry-making, Roberta lost her dread of what the new year might bring.

At suppertime, she found herself next to Marie. Marie had her eyes fixed on someone. Roberta followed her gaze. Muir.

Marie said: "Magnificent animal, isn't he?"

Mentally, Roberta curled her lip. Perhaps Marie hadn't changed so much after all. That was all men were to women like her, male counterparts to their own femininity.

"I think," she said gently, "there is more to Muir than that."

Marie nodded. "Of course. That was a stupid thing to say. Why – 'Romeo's a dish-clout to him.' "

Roberta stared. Yes, Muir was right. Marie had depth now, and discrimination. A chill finger touched Roberta's heart. Marie was infinitely more dangerous this way. The other Marie Muir would have seen through. Muir had classed Marie with Mary, Queen of Scots; Marie had set him above Romeo.

Marie was still following Muir with her eyes, and Roberta's own gaze went to the knot of hair on Marie's neck. There, just above the shining knot, nestled a *paua* shell clip, winking in the light.

"How pretty that is," said Roberta, touching it.

Marie nodded. "Yes, it was made out of one of those shells we gathered at All Day Bay years ago . . . remember?"

Roberta remembered very well. Maybe Muir had them made up wholesale. No doubt the moments he had spent with her as the clock struck had all been part of his policy . . . and no doubt he had been wishing all the time he could have been with Marie.

But now she must bid everyone goodbye, see all the girls had escorts for the lonely roads home . . . it was best to be busy anyway.

Marie and Muir were among the last to leave. Muir was driving Marie back to the Home. Roberta suddenly remembered she was to ask Marie to New Year's Tea.

She caught up a wrap and sped light-footed over the dewy grass. Muir's car was still there, under the big gum. She came across to it, but could see no one inside it. Then she heard the murmur of low voices from the far side of the car in the shadow of the tree.

Marie's voice, with a note of anguish.

"I'm afraid to look forward into another year, Muir. It will be empty, like all the others."

Muir's voice, infinitely compassionate and tender:

"Oh, my dear, my dear. . . ."

Roberta's eyes had become accustomed to the darkness now, and she could see them faintly, the gleam of the pin in Muir's plaid, the shining satin of Marie's dress, the dark bar that was Muir's arm about her.

Roberta turned, without a betraying sound. As she went in through the great door, she laid a hand on the lintel ... Oh, Heatherleigh, Heatherleigh ... once it had known the happiness of a family, with Robert and Ishbel Heatherleigh, their three sons and one daughter; throwing their house wide to the estate workers, Hester and Robert, Dugald and Ian joining in the seasonal festivities. Now Grandy had but one small granddaughter, to carry on the old tradition, to break her heart because of them. There was no happiness under Heatherleigh's roof-tree any more ... only doubt, and intrigue and — what was it Marie had said? ... Emptiness. ...

CHAPTER EIGHT

SUDDENLY, it seemed, the festive season was over. The days were long and lovely, golden and blue. North Otago shimmered in the sun of near-drought days. This was a pausing time for the farms, but would be short this year, for the rush of the harvest would soon be upon them, owing to the dry conditions.

Roberta took full advantage of the leisurely time to lead Muir on, sensing that each day he grew more sure of her. They spent long days together in the saddle, at the river, bathing or fishing. Henk was away at Kakanui Beach with his aunt and cousins.

Roberta had gone over to cook dinner for Muir at his request. It had been a busier day for him, because the day before, he and Roberta had spent the whole time riding over the boundaries of the two estates, examining fences.

Roberta had seen him only once when he came over for the milk pails. She had been cooking then, baking cheese straws for their after-dinner coffee. When she had gone up to Muir's bedroom to change, she had looked in the bedside table. The miniature was there again, wrapped now in a soft silk handkerchief, yellow with age.

She hadn't brought anything elaborate to change into . . . it was to be just a simple farmhouse dinner, with the open windows of the dining-room looking out on to a field of red clover, ready for cutting.

Roberta was hot from bending over the stove, so she showered quickly, donned two brief garments, and slipped into a cool-looking green linen dress. She wore green sandals on her bare brown feet.

She brushed her hair with Muir's hairbrush till it shone, applied make-up rather sparingly – this weather gave one enough colour, anyway – and went out to put the finishing touches to the dinner table.

She had just set two perfect Peace roses, creamy yellow, flushed with cerise, in a glass jar in the centre of the table, and turned to see Muir in the doorway, watching her. She smiled back. Muir always demanded from her, somehow or other, an instinctive response. She must remember to subdue it . . . though it didn't matter — as yet.

Muir said, with confidence: "I'm hot and sticky, darling . . . I'll not kiss you till I change."

Darling! That, from a Scotsman, was as good as a proposal.

She was sitting at her place at the table, when he came back, bathed, and in light sports trousers and open-necked silk shirt. He came up behind her, turned her face up and kissed her. He put his cheek against hers.

"You look as cool as a water lily, love," he said.

Roberta reflected that she didn't feel cool . . . inwardly or outwardly.

It was a pleasant meal. Roberta had to remind herself several times that it was, after all, just makebelieve. There was nothing real about it, about the apparent affection on Muir's side, or on hers. For a moment, once, a deep regret touched her heart. If only it had been true . . . if only Muir Buchanan had loved her for herself, not for the acres she would inherit!

Muir looked up from carving himself another slice of cold chicken, and caught her expression, unguarded momentarily. He laid down the carving knife and fork, and caught her hand.

"What is it, little one?" he asked.

It was almost the undoing of Roberta. That had been what he had called her all those years ago when there had been no guile in him.

"What do you mean?" she asked.

He held her gaze, well aware she was stalling.

"There was a shadow in your eyes . . . there's something bothering you."

"Sheer imagination," she said.

He shook his head.

130

"It isn't. Some day you'll not hold things back from me, I hope."

Roberta rose.

"I'll bring in the sweets. I left them in the fridge till the last possible moment."

They had coffee before washing up. Muir said he wanted to settle down for the whole evening when they had done the dishes.

Muir went through to the drawing-room. He knew Roberta would follow him when she had washed her hands with scented soap that would dispel that dishpan feeling. He filled his pipe but didn't light it.

Outside, beyond the open french windows, Iceland poppies danced, and roses scattered petals and perfume far and wide. Great spikes of delphinium bloomed royally against the walls, and the rose arches were thick with crimson ramblers and briars.

Twilight was veiling the far hills in amethyst haze and birds were whistling sleepily down in the gully by the stream. Beyond the ranges lingered the afterglow of the sunset.

Roberta picked up a magazine from a small table as she came through. Muir took it from her and dropped it on to the big chintz-covered couch. She raised an eyebrow at him.

"Am I not allowed to relax with some light reading matter after all my labours cooking your dinner?"

He shook his head. She saw a smile lift the corners of his mouth.

"There are better things to do . . . this, for instance." He pulled her down with him to the couch, and gathered her close, looking at her with that in his eyes that she couldn't meet with her own. Not frankly. She looked down.

"Roberta," he said softly. "It's home to you too, isn't it, my dear one . . . Buchanan? I know it can't be compared to Heatherleigh, but it's mine, and I want you to share it with me. You will, won't you?"

She lifted her head and looked at him, her eyes, for once, expressionless.

131

"Why?" she asked.

For a moment, she thought, he looked puzzled, then it was as though he suddenly understood.

"— You want it in so many words . . . but you've known, you've known for a long time. It will take a lifetime for me to tell you properly. I love you, Roberta."

He went to gather her closer, but the small hand came up against his chest. He stopped, aware that there wasn't, in Roberta's eyes, just what he'd hoped for.

A voice that didn't sound like hers at all, but had a fine thread of amusement running through it, said:

"Are you really asking me to marry you, Muir Buchanan?"

Roberta's face was cold, her green eyes icy. There was scorn and amusement and a hint of venom in her expression.

Muir's mouth went grim.

"Just that!" he said, and waited.

"What makes you think I would?"

In silence he looked at her . . . as he had never looked at her before. She didn't like what she read in that look. Muir was no doubt remembering how she had tantalised George at the pool, and thought she was making a habit of it.

"You know why I thought you would," he said. "I'd never have believed you would have taken my lovemaking lightly. You knew I wasn't taking it lightly, didn't you? Didn't you, Roberta?"

She shrugged her shoulders and achieved a laugh.

"Aren't you taking a little delightful foolery rather seriously, Muir?"

"Yes," he said.

He came to his feet and pulled her to hers.

"Roberta, you did know I was going to ask you to marry me, didn't you?"

"No," she said.

His hands on her shoulders tightened till his fingers bit into her flesh. There were fiery sparks in his dark eyes.

"You lie!" he said. "You know perfectly well I would never have talked to any woman as I talked to you yesterday afternoon, unless I had thought I was going to spend the rest of my life with her in the most intimate relationship of all."

Roberta's head came up. There was still that hint of amusement in her tone that exasperated Muir.

"It would have been very difficult to head you off, Muir, once started."

He flushed darkly. Roberta had never seen him so evidently angry.

"Nonsense!" he said, and his voice was scornful and despising. It flicked her spirit like a whip. "Any woman can lead the conversation into the channels she approves of."

Roberta laughed. She hoped the laugh would hurt him.

"Men do deceive themselves . . . a statement like that is rather revealing . . . it tallies with the idea that it's up to women, and women alone, to preserve the standards of morality for the sake of the duty they owe to society!"

His fingers were still hurting her with the intensity of his grip.

"I think you're being rather cheap, Roberta. I've never subscribed to the idea that women, and women alone, have to preserve the standards of ordinary decency . . . but I still say you oughtn't to have let me go on talking like that, if you hadn't meant to marry me."

Misery and temper and all the frustrations of the past weeks rose up and overwhelmed Roberta.

"You make me laugh," she said. "I suppose I'm to feel honoured that you have sought my hand in marriage, but it's very difficult to feel honoured when you take it like this. . . . I'd always understood a woman could say: No, thank you! and it would be graciously accepted."

"Instead of which," said Muir, his lips a thin line, "I have behaved like a boor . . . which, after all, is only what your own behaviour merited. Besides all that," the words bit, "it's only what could be expected when a one-time shepherd aspires to the heiress of Heatherleigh, isn't it?"

"Exactly," agreed Roberta, the cruel finality of the word dropping like a chip of ice into a crystal bowl.

This was the moment when she had expected to feel triumph. She had paid Muir Buchanan out for all the humiliation of the bargaining conversations she had heard . . . but she knew no triumph . . . she only felt cheap.

She turned away. She said: "I'll just get my things and go."

He followed her into the bedroom. She caught up the apron and overall she had cooked the dinner in, and threw them into her case on top of her make-up kit and comb.

"Just a minute," said Muir.

He tugged open the drawer containing the miniature, drew it out, and dropped it on top of the apron.

"You might as well have this too," he said, and from his copy of Burns plucked a snapshot of Roberta and George, taken on the porch at Heatherleigh all those years ago.

"Thank you," said Roberta, in a small, polite voice, and snapped the case shut. He escorted her to the front door, wished her goodnight. He was very final.

Roberta saw her grandfather riding in the direction of Buchanan the next day, so she supposed Muir had phoned him to go over.

Old Robert didn't say anything to her till three days later. She did notice he had looked frailer and older and very tired. She had avoided the chance of solitary conversation with him, but had gone into the study with some papers that had been piling up on the dining-room mantelpiece. She thought the study was unoccupied. It wasn't. Her grandfather was at his desk.

"Oh, sit down, lassie," he said. He hesitated for a moment, fiddled with some papers, then looked up at her.

"So you're not going to marry Buchanan, after all?" he asked, watching her keenly.

Roberta's chin lifted.

"Did *you* think I was going to, too?"

"Aye," said old Robert, and sighed. Roberta could see that he was going to marshal up all sorts of arguments why she should. Grandy had mellowed, but at times was still very autocratic, and an ill man to cross, and this was very dear to his heart.

She looked at the old man with a weariness that caught at his heart had she but known it.

"Grandfather," she said, "you wouldn't want me to marry anyone I couldn't love . . . would you?"

Her grandfather looked searchingly. "No," he said simply. "I wouldn't like you to marry except for love. It's the only basis possible. It's just that . . ." He stopped, and went on, "Muir Buchanan is the finest man I know."

Roberta's lip curled.

"Don't you mean the finest farmer you know?"

The old eyes looked puzzled.

"Yes, that too, but what's that to do with it? Heatherleigh will be yours when I go, Roberta. You'll be a wealthy woman. I'd like to see you wed before I die. When I'm gone there won't be anyone to protect you from fortune-hunters."

Roberta closed her eyes for a moment. She supposed Grandy was deliberately shutting his eyes to the fact that he and Muir had deliberately planned this.

"What about George?" she asked. "Where does he come in?"

"I'm leaving George a legacy," said Robert. "In fact, keep this to yourself, but I've wondered this last little while if it wouldn't be better to settle a certain amount on George now, and let him go back to Australia. I'd rather not have him around."

Just then Roberta caught sight of Muir coming across the rose garden to the door.

She rose and left the room.

Muir came and went much as usual, but was more taciturn than of old. The drought continued, and the pastures were shrivelled and brown. Rain clouds piled up in the south-west, clinging to the hills about Palmerston South, circled westward about the Kakanuis, and came back eastward at Timaru, leaving North Otago in a hot, dry basin. The milk yield dropped, and the sheep were continually on the move, never lying placidly chewing.

Further out the small townships were desperate for water, as they depended solely on rainwater supplies. Wells were hard to sink in North Otago, and what water was brought up was hard because of the limestone nature of the ground.

Big trucks could be seen at all hours of the day pumping water from the river in huge tanks to be taken to where ever needed. At Ngpara they were paying ten dollars a tank for water. The time involved, and the distance carted, made it dear. Heatherleigh was one of the few townships that never knew a shortage of water. Robert and Ishbel had had pipes laid on to all the cottages from the river, and their paddocks were irrigated too.

Roberta spent long hours hosing the vegetables in the kitchen garden, to help the gardener, glad of the manual labour of mulching and hoeing.

The currants, black and red, ripened, as did the raspberries and strawberries. Roberta helped Meg and the children pick them, and bottle them or put them into jam.

The first of the apples, the Gravensteins, began to ripen, and the peaches against the studio window were now showing a tempting rosy glow. Meg was making large fruit cakes and shortbread and biscuits, things that would keep and come in useful when they began to harvest, and paddock lunches were the order of the day.

Muir was away for a few days. Roberta thought it might be Sydney again, and that he didn't want George to know. It was ridiculous really, for George was behaving beautifully. He had been most solicitous about Grandfather, taking him in to the doctor for a blood test check-up, driving the big De Soto. He wanted old Robert to get some sleeping pills, to help him get longer hours of rest, but Robert had all the old-timer's scorn of such things.

"I'll sleep well enough come harvest," he chuckled.

Muir was still away when the fire swept over from Koromiko Creek and threatened Heatherleigh. There were afforestation areas in the way, well surrounded by firebreaks, but the fire started the night before, the worst nor'wester of the season swept down upon them, a hot-breathed fury.

It was quite as bad as any nor'wester in mid-Canterbury, where they sweep down the river gorges of the Rangitata and Rakaia and scourge the plains. Nor'westers came across the Tasman, as moisture-laden gales, but dropped their rain on the watershed of the Alps and tore across the plains as a hot dry wind, driving clouds of dust and river silt into every homestead. North Otago got only the tail-enders as a rule, but this one hit them fairly and squarely.

The fire had a good hold before it was discovered, had raced through a whole plantation of pines, and one immense tree had fallen across the firebreak and reached far enough into the long grass on the far side to touch off some dry blue-gum leaves.

It was ten o'clock before word reached Heatherleigh. The men of Koromiko had been out since seven, but it had been some time before they realised the flames had jumped the firebreak.

Old Robert and Andy and MacGregor got the firefighters organised. Men came from everywhere, Tesche-makers, Maheno, Otepopo, Oamaru. Roberta and Meg and the two girls were flat out serving relays of tea and scones, driving the stuff out by Land-rover wherever needed to refresh the men. Mrs. Crossman from the Arms sent up trayloads of cakes and cut bread for sandwiches.

The wind was a personal enemy, driving the flames and sparks further and further into the trees and bush. Some of the men were rounding up the sheep in the far paddocks, working with speed and energy and unflagging grit in the pitiless heat and smoke.

The air was foul with the smell of burning and raucous with the cries of the men to the dogs as they rounded up sheep, and with the snapping and crackling of resinous leaves.

Roberta couldn't bear to see the little things of the wild fleeing desperately from the coverts that had given them shelter. She thought with pity of the fledglings who couldn't fly, the tiny rabbits deep in their burrows, the mothers who wouldn't leave them. She saw a stoat and a rabbit come out of the undergrowth together, away from the fire, neither of them aware that they ran together.

They prayed for a wind change ... If only it would go round to the sou'west. The glass was low, certainly, but then it always dropped for nor'westers. Roberta came back in the Land-rover, and decided to take Henk, who was with her, over to Buchanan to see if he could manage the milking, with David's help.

Neither of the boys was happy at the thought of leaving the firefighting, but it looked as if it was getting under control now, and the men would be dead beat. Roberta didn't know much about milking machines, but if the boys showed her how the cups went on, she could help.

It wasn't till they ran the Land-rover into the milking yard that they saw the advancing cloud of smoke from over the far hill. Roberta sat at the wheel, aghast. Trees led right to Buchanan from that hill, and down the other side.

The grass was fairly short around the homestead, but the trees came close to shelter the garden. One spark could set it going. All Muir had put into the property for years would be doomed. The firefighters were too far away ... two to three miles from here. She would have to go back over the cutting, and through the yards at Heatherleigh, with all the gates to open, and right through the homestead to find them. Besides, she didn't think they would be able to leave the other blaze yet.

As they watched, Roberta saw the foliage of an enormous wattle burst into a ball of flame. It burnt out in a few moments, and a bunch of leaves tossed into the air and landed in a huge macrocarpa; she heard the crackling as it too caught. There were dozens of macrocarpas there, and the clippings from the hedges were always burnt green as they contained methylated spirits and were easy to dispose of.

She turned to the boys.

"Henk, you can drive the Rover, can't you? Well, you

138

know there were transport men at the swing bridge pumping water earlier this afternoon? Drive very carefully, for heaven's sake, and see if they are still there, and get them to come at once. Tell them to bring their trucks as near as they can, and the tanks, and I'll have plenty of sacks up there ready to soak. If they shouldn't be there, go to the village.''

She turned the Land-rover for the boys, saw an excited Henk take the wheel, and said a silent prayer for their safety, then rushed into the grain shed for sacks and axes and shovels. She must do what she could till the men got there. She flung them into the back of Muir's old utility truck, backed it out of its shed, and wound round the track towards the hillside.

It was nine o'clock, and just dark when Muir returned. The wind had changed at five, swung around to the sou'west, and now rain was falling steadily, had been for two hours, and all danger was over.

Even the milking had been done. The transport men had finished the bacon and eggs Roberta had cooked for them, and were sitting back in the big, bare kitchen, smoking. Henk was soaking blissfully in a bath, and Roberta had promised to spend the night in the house. He was much too tired to pack off to his aunt's house.

She was going to go and tidy up in a moment when the men left. She had been too achingly tired and hungry and thirsty to do so before. Now she felt she would have just enough stamina to last till they had gone. Then she would pile the dishes in the sink, attend to the dirt and scars upon her, and tumble into bed.

The kitchen was as filthy as the firefighters. There was charcoal and mud, twigs, leaves, and ash all over the floor. Their one need had been for food, and now, for rest.

Roberta had towelled her soaking hair dry, but had not combed it, tying it back with a bootlace she had picked up. Her shirt was torn and filthy, her cardigan a mass of charred holes, and her slacks, once green corduroy, beyond hope and decency.

139

Muir was immaculate in city clothes, in direct contrast to the four in the kitchen.

It sounded as if Henk was rushing to get out of the bath and into pyjamas so he could tell Muir all about it. Naturally he'd be dying to tell the whole thing — after all the times Muir had warned him not to drive yet on the roads, but keep to the tracks through the paddocks, he would enjoy relating that he'd actually been ordered to.

It was half an hour before Henk could be persuaded to bed. Fortunately Muir had bought him a book in Christchurch. It might calm him to read a little while.

While Roberta was seeing him into bed, Muir thanked the transport men, and gave them a cheque each for their help and their ruined clothing.

Roberta came back into the kitchen, shut the door, and leaned against it, looking at Muir.

He came across to her, towering above her.

"So you saved Buchanan for me?"

Roberta said nothing. She was too deadly tired for anything.

"Why did you?" asked Muir. There was something inexorable about him, something she couldn't fight at the moment . . . but she must.

Muir continued: "After all, Buchanan means nothing to you . . . you ought to have been at Heatherleigh. It wasn't out of danger."

Roberta leaned her head back against the door. But she mustn't let the weakness of the flesh betray her. It would be so easy to say: "Because Buchanan is yours." But she mustn't, she mustn't. Muir must never suspect she loved him . . . Muir who really loved Marie, yet was willing to sacrifice her too for the sake of acquiring the estate. She shut her eyes against the fierce, compelling gaze, then opened them and said flatly: "Don't you realise why I fought the flames at Buchanan, Muir? — Because if your house had caught, there would have been nothing to stop the pines on the east side of the garden catching alight. They lead right up the hill and down to that part where the river is narrowest . . .

a tree falling there would have set our trees alight, and Heatherleigh would have been doomed. *That's why I saved Buchanan!*"

Muir stepped forward, gripped her by the shoulders. As his grasp burst the blisters under the ragged shirt, she cried out with pain, and slowly slid to the floor.

Muir looked down at her, aghast, his fingers sticky with the oozing blisters.

She came to almost immediately, and sat up.

"I did *not* faint . . . it was just tiredness," she said crossly.

"All right," he said. "It was just tiredness. I've got an excellent first-aid kit here. I'll get Meg over and she can help me dress the wounds." He pulled up the torn leg of her slacks, and whistled as he saw the ugly scratches and burns.

Roberta said, getting to her feet, "You can take me over home. Meg can attend to them over there."

Muir said flatly: "You are not going outside again on a night like this. You could get a chill, and it might do the burns untold damage. Besides, there's bound to be a certain amount of shock. I'll get Meg to stay the night."

It was like fighting a feather pillow to protest more.

As Muir came back from the phone Henk came running out.

"What's in this other parcel, Muir?"

"Oh, a spare part for your meccano. Marie sent it to you. I called at the orphanage on the way home. It was she who told me there was a fire out this way. Now off to bed. Roberta's burns are nasty, and Meg is coming over. Lights out right away, Henk."

He turned to Roberta.

"Roll your sleeves up, will you? I'll get your arms bandaged before Meg arrives, then she can take over."

Roberta submitted to his ministrations, inwardly seething, conscious all the while of his touch, and her heart thudding against her ribs. Reaction, she told herself, after hours of unresting physical action, and superficial burns.

Muir went ahead with the calm efficiency that was so

much a part of him, cleansing, and applying soothing compresses.

Roberta said: "You have quite a few surprising accomplishments ... I didn't realise such expert first-aid was amongst them."

Muir replied: "Of course it is. Living here in the country, so far from a doctor, even with the speed of modern transport one needs to know how to cope with most things."

Polite conversation ... filling in time till Meg should get here. There would be more small-talk then, with Meg trying to keep things on a normal footing, knowing there was enmity between them. She was just as bad as Grandy in wishing things different, and almost as transparent.

Roberta awoke to a sunlit morning, fresh after last night's rain. She looked across to Meg's bed. Meg was fast asleep, her head pillowed on her arm, a faint smile playing around her lips. Roberta wondered if in her dreaming she walked with John, as of old. At least Meg had happy remembrances, and trust and faith.

Roberta had an idea she would be wise to get away home as soon as possible. She rose, and quietly, though stiffly, dressed. Meg woke just as she was finished. She sat up, yawning.

"Heavens, what energy! You must be very resilient, Roberta ... here am I, still flat out, and I wasn't half as weary as you, nor have I a single burn."

"I thought we'd get away to Heatherleigh as soon as you're ready, Meg. We can wash properly over there. It will be a busy morning."

Roberta went out of the room. She could hear Muir moving about. She would just call out, casually, that they were on their way.

He came out of his room, fully dressed, and raised his brows at sight of her.

"Meg's almost ready," she said. "I'm just going to get the car out."

"You're not going without breakfast," said Muir.

They measured glances.

"There will be a lot to do over at the big house," said Roberta. "It's in a terrible mess after yesterday. There was no time to do anything last night, Meg tells me."

Back in the bedroom, Meg, who had heard every word of this, was on the point of calling out that it really didn't matter, she would have all day to cope with it, and that the girls had promised to be there early, but she decided against it. Better leave them to it.

Muir said, expressionlessly: "You're staying here for breakfast. After that I'm taking you in to Oamaru to the doctor. My first-aid is only of the amateur variety, and I want expert opinion on your burns."

"No need for that, I can assure you. They're purely superficial."

"They may be, but I want assurance of that from someone who knows. I want no infection to set in."

Roberta uttered a sound of pure scorn.

Now there was impatience in his voice.

"People who insist on being spartan are simply nuisances to themselves and to others. They pride themselves on not making a fuss, and then in the end they cause a deal more bother, by getting into serious trouble."

Roberta lost her temper.

"You — you. . . !" She visibly controlled herself.

Muir said: "You have put Buchanan in your debt, and I must see you come to no harm by it."

What did he mean by Buchanan? The estate, or the man? Oh, undoubtedly the estate . . . it was all he cared about.

Her voice bit. "It would be a pity if you were under an obligation to anyone, wouldn't it? You take no help from anyone, do you? You haven't much time for faults and weaknesses. A sort of superman. Always so righteous, so self-sufficient. No need of me, or anyone else!"

Muir said: "You're wrong there, you know. I had a need of you. You should know that."

It twisted the knife in her wounds. Yes, a need of what I

bring you . . . never a need of *me*. She turned on her heel and went into the kitchen.

Meg emerged from the bedroom, cautiously. She looked at Muir.

"I couldn't help overhearing, Muir. I think I'll sneak off to Heatherleigh right now, and leave the two of you to work it out."

He smiled, grimly. "There's nothing left to work out."

She said: "You're right . . . about the burns. Get her in to the doctor. I'll slip out by the side door. I don't want to argue with her."

"Good for you, Meg," he said, and touched her hand in thanks.

He went in to the kitchen, after using the phone.

"The doctor is seeing us at a quarter to nine before he sets out on his rounds, Roberta, so we'd better step on it."

Roberta was glad Henk was there for breakfast, chattering at top speed, quite unaware that there was something wrong in the grown-ups' world this morning.

"These things aren't very smart for town," said Roberta, surveying her linen dress and cardigan.

"It doesn't matter," said Muir. "It will be just in and out again. If I let you off at Heatherleigh to change, you're perverse enough to give me the slip and get away to the doctor in your own car."

Roberta had thought that very thing. She compressed her lips and said nothing.

As they pressed the bell at the doctor's residence and walked into the waiting-room, she said distantly:

"I don't suppose I'll be long. Your favourite reading matter is there."

She indicated a pile of magazines with *The Scotsman* lying on top.

Muir said calmly: "I'm coming in with you to make sure you show the doctor all the injuries. You're in such a stupid mood you'll probably minimise them if I don't!"

They heard a chuckle behind them, and turned to find the doctor. He knew them both, Muir the better, of course.

144

Roberta said, not caring: "I will not minimise them. You have had your own way this morning far more than is good for you, Mr. Buchanan, and besides, there are a few burns I couldn't show you last night . . . so you will stay right here!"

The doctor chuckled again. "Fighting like a pair of kids," he admonished. "I've just settled a squabble like this at my own breakfast table." He put a hand on Roberta's shoulder, and said to Muir: "Don't worry, I'll make her tell all," and ushered her into the surgery. Roberta felt inordinately pleased.

Expert attention made her feel much easier, and the doctor handed Muir a prescription for tablets to ward off infection. They had to wait a few minutes for them. While they waited, Muir said to Roberta: "I brought in some mail to post. It won't take a moment."

He stopped at the post office.

"It's in the door pocket on your side, Roberta. Would you hand it to me?"

The mail consisted of one letter. Roberta's grip wasn't secure because of the bandaging, but that wasn't what made her drop it.

The letter was to Marie. The address stared up at her in the black positive writing that was so typical of Muir . . . a fat, bulging letter, that had needed cellotape on the flap to seal it.

So . . . tired as Muir had been last night, and late though the hour, he must have sat down and written pages to Marie . . . and a letter as thick as that, written under those conditions, could be none other than a love letter.

Marie was only in Oamaru, at the end of a telephone, and he had seen her just last night. But there were things you couldn't say over a party line . . . tender, foolish things. . . .

The journey back home was accomplished in silence.

Muir came in to see Robert, and Roberta and he parted at the study door.

"Thank you," said Roberta. "Now you need feel no more responsibility towards me."

But Muir made no reply.

It was just as well there was so much to do. Roberta flung herself into the seasonal work in the house, making jams and bottling fruit and berries. She couldn't do much outdoor work, as the burns were too tender for riding.

The men were busy too, at first keeping watch over the smouldering logs that could so easily dry out too soon, and clearing away the traces of the fire as much as possible, though the black scars on the lovely hillsides must remain till nature herself clothed them again with green.

"It will mean a lot of replanting," said Muir. "North Otago hasn't half the trees it should have to stop erosion and give shelter. Of course the heat will have germinated thousands of pine and wattle seeds. But after harvest we must have a planting-out programme organised on a large scale."

At the end of January Meg and Roberta and the children went to Kakanui for a week at the seaside. Grandy insisted on it.

"You've been pale ever since the fire," he said.

Meg smiled to herself. It was really Muir who had done the insisting. She had overheard him say to Grandfather, "But don't tell her I recommended it."

Then the harvest was upon them, and strangely enough the tension they all felt seemed to slacken in the need for hard physical work, and the goal of finishing the task. George was working well, better than he had ever done, and there were fewer trips to Dunedin for him. Roberta had an idea that George's trips down south were to hit the high spots; he had the look of it when he returned. However, they evidently didn't have the same attraction as before.

When the harvest work slackened a little there was still plenty of fruit to make use of, in the orchard.

"I think we'll get in the last of the apricots and nectarines today," said Meg.

Roberta said: "All right ... but don't think I'm getting browned off with the job when I say that I had an idea you

146

weren't going to do any more, and that you said the shepherds' wives could have the rest."

"They had all they wanted that day you spent entirely up in the studio. Then they have a few trees, younger ones, on their own places." She hesitated, and added: "These are for Buchanan. I offered to do some for Muir."

Roberta said hastily: "Oh, well, count me out. That wouldn't enthrall me at all." A wicked gleam came into her eye. "But I believe it's Marie's day off. Why don't you ring her up and ask if she would like to help?"

She looked up to see Muir standing in the doorway. Now how long had he been there? She didn't care.

Muir said, ignoring Roberta, "I came over to see if you wanted a hand to pick the fruit, Meg. Some of those trees should have been pruned more severely in their youth, and I've got a longer reach."

Meg said: "I'd love you to help, but I've a free afternoon, and the children will lend a hand later, so if you have anything else more urgent, Muir, don't bother. I'll manage."

"I want to see Mr. Heatherleigh afterwards," said Muir, "and he told me he wouldn't be free till half-past three. I'll fill in time picking till then, Meg."

Meg picked up a couple of baskets and said over her shoulder to Roberta: "Be a dear and make me a batch of scones for tea . . . and if you'd like to make the three o'clock cuppa I'd be grateful."

Roberta was left feeling decidedly cross, in the hot kitchen. It was too bad of Meg . . . sheer devilment on her part, to punish her for refusing to help with Muir's preserves.

She made the scones and prepared a dainty afternoon tea, although she felt she would have enjoyed it more had Muir not been coming in for it. It was most exasperating the way Meg and Grandy ignored the state of warfare between the two of them, going on including Muir in all plans, and in general treating them like a couple of children who had quarrelled and were sulking. Roberta was glad when she had her trips to Auckland, and sometimes stayed longer up there than she need.

Grandy came in and joined them, savouring the cool cucumber sandwiches and custard squares. He took a round of bread, chilled in the refrigerator, and filled with a delightful concoction of salmon and gherkins, then cut into wheels.

"I'm not sure they are good for my eighty-year-old digestion," he said, "but there are worse ways to die."

Muir said: "Something to be said for having a domestic science expert to run your house for you, sir."

Meg said, with honesty, "It was Roberta who taught me to make those. In fact, I owe her a lot of recipes . . . all those Continental dishes and sauces. Have one, Muir?"

"No, thank you," he said gravely. "I'm allergic to gherkins."

Roberta rather hoped the cucumber would disagree with him too.

Muir said as Grandy finished his second cup of tea: "Can you spare me a few moments now, sir?" He turned at the door and added: "I'm not dodging, Meg, I'll be back to help you stone the fruit."

As Roberta heard the study door close behind them she wondered if there would ever come a time when Heatherleigh would be free of Muir Buchanan. Not in Grandy's time, she supposed, for nothing could come between those two men, but when she was Heatherleigh's mistress Muir Buchanan should not set foot in the place!

Roberta washed the tea dishes for Meg, then, as soon as she heard Muir returning, said she must be off to the studio.

Later, from her window, she watched him going away. Doss at his heels, and something in his bearing, and the way he was whistling: "Gan on the forty-second, gan on the forty-twa . . ." suggested triumph. Now what had Muir Buchanan to feel triumphant about at the moment?

The next day she realised why Muir had looked so pleased with himself. George came up to her studio where she was busy drawing.

"Have you heard about the land over the river . . . beyond Yellowstone Ford?"

"Heard what? That they're going to put more of it in wheat? It's no use making a fuss about that, George, I went into that pretty thoroughly myself, and only succeeded in making a fool of myself. They're doing that because they have a conscience on the matter. We ought to produce more wheat."

"I don't mean that at all . . . I mean that it no longer belongs to Heatherleigh. Muir has bought it."

Roberta dropped her pencil, and came across to George.

"You don't mean *all* of it? Not the stretch right from the Ford to the boundary?"

"I do. It's all signed and sealed. No hope of putting a spoke in the wheel. There's as much ground there as at Buchanan."

Roberta knew dismay. She spoke before she thought.

"This is his way of hitting back!"

George said, on a puzzled note: "What do you mean?"

She flushed, but knew she would have to answer. "Because I wouldn't marry him," she said.

George took one look at her stricken face and left her.

Roberta faced it out. Muir Buchanan was no man to be easily turned from his purpose. He was a vindictive man, and he had a knack of getting what he wanted.

There was nothing she could do about it. Where Muir was concerned, Grandy was adamant. He trusted Muir to the limit. Old people were like that. The opinions they formed in their earlier life just couldn't be changed. Besides . . . Roberta had no ambition to do anything about it. Disillusion had withered up everything that mattered.

During the long watches of the night, when she switched on her light and read till the small hours to tire herself to the point of sleep, she came to grips with the situation. There would be less left for her.

No doubt Grandy, failing a little, wouldn't drive as hard a bargain on land prices as his executors would. In time Buchanan would be larger than Heatherleigh. Muir would probably bring Marie to it some day, and Roberta would live on at Heatherleigh, alone.

Or would she? Or would she cut free again, footloose, to travel, and this time to know no stint of money? She didn't know. What could she bear most easily ... the loss of Heatherleigh, or the sight of Muir and Marie in their happiness together? Roberta couldn't answer this, even to herself. Her sole consolation was that Marie had been transferred back to Wellington.

Roberta was taking Clancy over to the smithy at Koromiko Creek when full proof of Muir's craftiness burst upon her. She had taken the short cut to the Koromiko Road, avoiding the bridge, because the less chance of encountering Muir the better, and fording the river at Yellowstone.

This was a lovely part of the estate ... now Buchanan's. The thought was bitter. She thought back to Grandy telling her how he had ceased to be land-hungry when Grandmother, the lovely Ishbel, had lain at death's door with diphtheria. The estate had certainly got whittled down since then. Odd that even now Grandy couldn't realise that Muir was acquisitive.

Clancy picked her way carefully, then they came out on to the road. Roberta delighted in its winding turns and leafy hollows where the road surface was a shifting mosaic of leaf shadow and sunshine.

To the left the road was bordered by a high ridge with weathered limestone outcroppings set on the sharp skyline and with gnarled *ngaios* leaning out from it. Further on the ridge was less rocky, and, turning a bend, she saw signs of unusual activity ... tractors and bulldozers and excavators, busy on the flatter surface under the hill. What in the world could they be doing?

She rode up and asked the foreman: "What goes on here?"

He put his hand in his pocket, drew out a packet of cigarette papers and some tobacco and began to roll a cigarette.

"We're preparing the ground for a limeworks. The

buildings will be here. Small fortune in lime up on that ridge."

Roberta hid her sickening sense of dismay, chatted easily to the man, and rode on.

Grandy was easy prey for Muir, age must be dimming his judgment all right . . . She thought of Grandy refusing to open up the ridge of lime above the Pool of Darkness because the natural beauty of the estate would be spoiled by a road being cut through and a white scar gashed into the hillside . . . but those things didn't matter to Muir. There was only one thing she could do . . . ignore it. She would not give him the satisfaction of triumphing openly over his latest deal.

She hoped that when next she saw Muir nothing might tempt her into betraying her knowledge of this, but he did not come near. She was dusting the study when Grandy came in.

He said: "Oh, I forgot. Muir told me to ask you if you would take Henk in to the dental clinic tomorrow. He's got a couple of fillings, and Muir didn't want to postpone it because it's hard to get another appointment soon."

"Why isn't Muir taking him himself?"

Her grandfather looked surprised.

"Didn't you know? Buchanan is in Australia. I thought you knew. Didn't he tell you himself?"

She shook her head.

"I've not seen him much this last week. In fact, not at all, I think. Is it more stud buying and selling?"

"Mostly. He's doing a bit of other business too."

Odd, since she oughtn't to care any longer, that it should hurt that Muir hadn't told her, or bidden her a goodbye, however casual it might have been.

She said, her voice hard, "And is it all hush-hush this time too? I mean, have we to keep it a secret from George?"

"No. Doesn't matter now. George has settled down."

She could be glad of that. She said: "Yes, I'll take Henk in."

Stupid, when there was no friendliness between her and

Muir when he was home, to find the days so long. She was glad to go out with George, down to Heatherleigh Arms. once into the cinema at Oamaru; fishing and riding.

One afternoon, after a particularly fruitless spell of fishing, they were having afternoon tea on the slope above the Pool of Darkness.

"I think we ought to call it the Pool of the Wily Old Salmon," said George. "I don't think we'll ever catch him. I'm going to Dunedin tomorrow on business. Grandy's going to let me have the truck."

Roberta said hastily: "George, don't get into any mischief, will you? I mean, Grandy is — is quite pleased with you just now ... don't do anything to jeopardise anything he might do for you."

"What do you mean?"

Roberta thought she had better take the plunge.

"Have you ever fancied setting up in some business of your own? A garage, or a farm implements agency? Or starting out on a farm of your own?"

"Yes. Often. But I haven't got the capital."

She said: "I rather think Grandy would help you with the finance if you wanted to do that. He admires initiative, you know, and if you fancied it, and were prepared to work hard, I'm sure he'd help."

"To the tune of what?" demanded George harshly.

"Oh, three or four thousand, I suppose."

George laughed shortly, and moved restlessly.

"The accident of birth," he said, and there was a sneer in his voice. "Aren't you glad you're a direct descendant? You get the lot!"

Now it was out in the open, at last. George had resented all along that she was Grandy's heiress. It hurt. This had been why she hadn't found George all she had hoped to find him.

Money! If it hadn't been for the money, George wouldn't be hanging around here, waiting for Grandy to die, so that the legacy that was in Grandy's original will should be his.

She turned to George, her eyes bitter.

152

"I hate money," she said. "Mother and Daddy were far happier without it. Mother never wanted to come home to share in it. She was perfectly happy and contented without it. When Daddy sold a picture we lived like kings . . . when he didn't we were all poor together, and I . . . I longed for Heatherleigh, for security, such as it is. How mad I must have been! We lived in some odd places, had some odd friends . . . but at least you knew why people liked you!"

George said, his eyes shrewd; "So that's why you turned Buchanan down? You thought he was after Heatherleigh."

He was sorry the next instant. The colour had left Roberta's face completely. It sounded even more horrible in someone else's words. She turned away from him, and hid her face on her arm.

Suddenly George's arm was about her. Something was in his voice she hadn't heard for years. Something young and sincere.

"I'm sorry, Roberta."

He kept his arm about her till she finished weeping. Then she sat up.

He said: "I'd not realised how hard it's been for you. I've not made it any easier for you, either. I've resented the fact that you will inherit Heatherleigh. I've been a bit of a fool, Roberta. It has always been in the back of my mind that I might inherit Heatherleigh some day. It has kept me from making the most of my chances at other things. I've been sort of filling in time." He hesitated, and said gently: "You love Muir, don't you? You always did."

She nodded. "But I found I couldn't marry on those terms, George."

He nodded. "There's nothing I can do to help you, Roberta, only let's be pals the way we used to be."

She put her hand in his and let him pull her to her feet.

She felt at peace for the first time for weeks. Life wasn't perfect, but there were things to be getting on with, you mightn't be able to face the future and the empty years, but somehow you found the courage to live a day at a time.

Tomorrow she would be on her own most of the day. She

was glad of that. Grandy and Meg were going in to Oamaru, Meg driving the De Soto, so there were just the two of them for lunch, she and George. Helen and Nancy had been given the day off. Grandy and Meg had asked her to go in with them, but she had refused.

"I feel like solitude," she said. "I'll give George an early lunch, he wants to be away by one. Anything you want me to do?"

"Just take this mail across to Buchanan and leave it on Muir's desk," said Grandy. "He asked me to attend to the estate stuff. These are personal letters."

After George had left, Roberta scooped them up. None from Marie, anyway.

Buchanan had the air of a house whose master is away. It was rather dusty, though no doubt Mrs. van Wyngen would be over tomorrow to prepare it for his homecoming. Roberta didn't linger. She went into the office and laid the letters down on his chair while she made room on his blotter for them.

His desk was unusually untidy. He had loose pages of a scribbling pad all over it. It looked as if he had been trying to compose something, for he had made endless starts. Roberta looked at them curiously, unaware that she was prying. He'd been ringing up a telegram, that was evident. The address was written on the top of the first one . . . Marie's.

Grandy had said Muir was going by flying-boat this time . . . of course, the flying-boats went from Wellington. Roberta suddenly realised now that she was prying, and didn't care. She picked them up, one after another.

The first one read: "Delightful coincidence. Will be in Wellington tomorrow." He had discarded that in favour of another, scrawling a pencil through the first. The second one read: "Timing excellent. Simply overjoyed. See you to-morrow," and the last one, at least she imagined it was the last, because it contained a definite time: "Delighted. With you in spirit today, in person tomorrow. See you at noon."

Roberta found she was shaking. She picked up the yellow leaflets, crushed them between her fingers, dropped them in the wastepaper basket. Oh, she shouldn't have done that, now Muir would know she had seen them, had been guilty of prying. Oh, well, he had a poor opinion of her now, so what odds? Or perhaps he would think Henk's aunt had done it. Anyway Roberta didn't care.

Back at Heatherleigh she saddled Clancy and rode away to the Pool of Darkness, all the way conscious that in those telegrams Muir had betrayed the depth of feeling that lay at the core of every Scot, something she herself had never been able to stir in him.

CHAPTER NINE

THE sun was gloriously hot, in fact, she was glad when it occasionally went behind the clouds, great cotton-wool puffs of cloud that piled up behind the hills down south. Not that they meant anything. Day after day since the fire they had watched the same thing and nothing had come of it.

The heat was becoming oppressive. It was a good thing she had tethered Clancy in the shade. Perhaps it would rain after all ... those clouds looked like thunder-clouds, she thought, though they were so far away it wouldn't come soon. She looked over her shoulder at the Kakanuis.

There, in the folds of the foothills, were little curls of cloud, wider at the base, and thinning out to a narrow neck. She smiled, remembering Muir's old swagger who had talked about "The whisky bottles on the foothills." Perhaps they would have rain by nightfall. They certainly needed it.

This sun was heavenly. It shone right through you, almost even warming your heart. But not quite. Roberta shook herself free of unwelcome brooding. She stretched herself out on the bank, her arms crossed, and her head pillowed on them. Why couldn't she feel as sleepy as this at night?

In the meantime, there was no hurry. She would have forty winks. Meg and Grandy had said they would just like a cold tea when they came in. They would have dinner in town at midday. The children would be in late today too. They had gone by bus to Palmerston South for some sports fixture. She had put a cold sweet and some icecream in the refrigerator for them. Suddenly Roberta was over the edge of sleep, sliding into blissful forgetfulness, where for once her doubts and heartaches did not follow to haunt her dreams. ...

She woke, not knowing where she was, and cold. Why, it was almost night, it was practically dark. Then she realised it was black with storm, such a storm as she had never known before. Since coming back to Heatherleigh, she had watched once, with Muir, a most spectacular electrical storm away back in the mountains, a weird, thrilling sight. But now she was right in the storm centre, alone, and that was a very different matter.

A vivid flash of lightning split the indigo sky, and Clancy screamed with terror. Roberta would have to go for her life to get home before the deluge that would follow. She half turned to get up just as the noise of the thunder reached the earth. Simultaneously came a closer sound . . . the sound of the mighty *totara* tree that had its roots among the limestone crags cracking . . . split from top to bottom by the lightning.

It fell, its topmost branches striking the Balancing Rock. The great rock pivoted, swayed from side to side, then crashed down the hillside, taking with it a great mass of limestone.

Roberta saw it coming before she had quite got on to her feet. There was only one thing to do; not that she reasoned it out, it was purely instinctive. She made a desperate effort to slip under the lee of the bank by the Pool before the rock could reach her, but as she slid over the edge the mass of rock caught up with her and they went over together. . . .

This time, when Roberta came cloudily back to consciousness, the darkness was the darkness of night, utter and complete. She knew fear and an intense loneliness. Somewhere around her water sucked and gurgled, and there was danger in that, and threat. Her mind suddenly cleared to a realisation of her position.

She was still here, by the Pool of Darkness, and it was late, and they hadn't found her. She was cold as she had never been cold before, and wet. She tried to turn, and an agonising pain stabbed at her right leg. . . . Broken? Crushed? . . . Well, certainly crushed, but worse than that, this was nightmare, only not a nightmare you could wake up from to find all terror fled, safe in your own bed, but an enduring one from which there might be no escape at all. She was caught like an animal in a trap, half in, half out of the Pool of Darkness, and her foot was buried in shingle under a huge mass of limestone, while the pitiless rain was soaking her, had been for hours presumably.

Hours of rain . . . a terrifying thought caught at Roberta's mind, blotting out temporarily the pain in her leg. Rain would be pouring down the foothills into the gullies, swelling the river till it reached flood level . . . in the last flood, Muir had said, the water had been well over the banks at the Pool, bringing down whole trees, and dead carcasses. . . . Muir! Muir wasn't home. He was probably winging across the Tasman at the moment, safe and secure in some huge, modern aircraft.

But the others would be organising a search party. She must tell herself that, mustn't succumb to panic. She thought of the vastness of the area that they must cover, and her heart failed her. They mightn't think of the river, they would miss Clancy, and come to the conclusion that she had been thrown. Oh, poor Grandy, it would bring back Dugald's death. . . .

She tried desperately to think what she had said to anyone about what she might do today. . . . George might know, she might have said to George she'd have a try to get a salmon, but she couldn't remember. Besides, would George be home yet? How long had he been going to stay in Dunedin? But surely, surely, some time in this black horrible pit of the night, someone would come here, they must, they must! She mustn't lose consciousness again, for they might ride by, calling her name.

Would Clancy break away, or had she already gone, terror of the lightning and thunder giving her strength to break away? Roberta felt she had broken away, for she felt alone. Her head was clearer now. She leant on an elbow, the stones cutting cruelly into her flesh, and tried to sit up. She couldn't, quite, but her eyes were getting used to the darkness now, and she could make out the outline of the limestone. With a straining, sweating effort, despite the cold in her bones, she reached down into the water with a sideways movement that was agony, to get her hand down to her ankle. It seemed to be embedded in shingle. That might have saved it from the full weight of the rock.

For the first time Roberta felt a stirring of hope. Perhaps there might be a slender chance that she could free herself. If only she could crawl up the bank, away from the menace of the rising water. She struggled to an easier position, and managed to get her hand under the ankle, scrabbling hastily at the shingle, feeling a little of it move, and the water sucking into the tiny hollow she had made. Then cramp attacked her, a searing, paralysing cramp in the hips. She had to assume her original position with haste. Again and again she tried, with the same results. It was no use.

Roberta suddenly realised something. The water was up to her waist now ... it had been only to her hips before, hard to be sure, with the rain still beating, but ... she put out a hand and encountered some larger pieces of limestone. She arranged them a few inches above the edge of the water. It would act as a guide to the rising of the water.

Suddenly Roberta became aware of something ... the rain had ceased. Not that it would matter to the rising of the river, for the water would still be streaming down the watershed of the hills, and if rescue didn't come soon, the water would be up to her throat. She struggled around again, reached down to the shingle, knew a tearing pain in her leg, then nothing more. . . .

Then she knew she was dreaming ... at least she must be dreaming ... because hands were running over her face, over her wet body, hands gentle but urgent, seeking to know the extent of her injuries ... a voice calling her name over and over ... Muir's voice.

She heard her own voice say weakly, a mere thread of sound, "It *is* you, isn't it? But it can't be, can it? Because you're in Sydney ... it couldn't be, could it?"

His breath was warm in her ear, and she had known no warmth of any kind for hours.

"It *is* me. I *am* here. You're safe now, safe."

His voice changed, became urgent.

"I've got to get you out of this. I can't leave you and go for help. I'll get something to lever this up with, and you must help. All my effort will be on prising the rock off your foot, I can't drag you away too . . . you'll have to put your hands on the shingle, and make a most terrific effort to get your foot out, and back."

"I'll try," said Roberta.

Muir said: "You'll not only try, you'll do it. You've got to."

She saw him scramble up the back, a fitful moon was gleaming out now behind the clouds; she saw him slip on something that glinted silver. The salmon. He muttered something, then stooped to pick up a log, tested it for rottenness, found it sound.

He stepped into the water beside her, looked all around the rock, measuring distance with his eye, testing the way it was likely to topple.

"If I lever it with the flow of the water, the very force of the stream may help it move," he said.

"Be careful, Muir, it may be scoured out there . . . don't step down into a pothole."

His answer was quick and reassuring, and he was back at her side. He propped her hands so that they would give her greatest leverage, then took up the log, and inserted it under a ledge on the great rock. His leg was braced against her hip, that would be to shield her as much as possible should the rock swing back, she guessed.

Muir drew in a deep breath and heaved, letting his breath run out. The rock moved, swung away from the leverage of the log. Muir dropped it, and as the rock settled back on her foot, he held it back with his arms, taking some of the weight but not all.

He swore, fluently, in the broadest Scots. Odd, for Muir had the reputation of being one of the few men about to manage even the dogs without swearing at them. Then, grimly, he picked up the log again.

"We've got to do it this time, Roberta."

The effort was almost beyond him, but inch by straining inch he moved it. Suddenly there was a giving, and Roberta, pinned in the river bed, felt stark fear lest it swing and crash on to her body. Muir's knee came up, pivoting the rock in the direction he wanted it, and with a mighty splash it toppled into the water.

Roberta had acted instantly. She felt the leg free itself from the loose shingle, no longer pressed down, and at the same moment, as the water rushed in gurgling and sucking, Muir bent to her, dragging her clear.

He sat down with her, cradled her head on his shoulder, and held her close, his wet face against hers. Roberta was aware of a multitude of things, relief, thankfulness, an unbearable pain in her foot, and a warmth in her heart that had nothing whatever to do with external cold. She was here, alive, and in Muir's arms ... not that it meant anything to him, to him she was merely a child at the moment, lost, and hurt, and in need of comfort. The pain rose up like a tide, swamping everything else. She moaned.

She saw Muir try to peer at the foot, wondering whether to move her or not, she supposed, then he got to his feet, picked her up, and struggled up the bank with her. Then he stood there, considering.

"I've got my horse here," he said, "but I don't like the thought of you going through the gullies, with your foot hanging over the saddle, it could do irreparable harm, but what ... ?"

She didn't know how long he considered it, she had lost count of time.

Then he said: "I know – the shepherd's hut. It's not a quarter of a mile away."

She didn't know how he got her on to the saddle, but he managed it somehow. He took off a scarf, wet and clinging, and bound her foot to the saddle, hurting her horribly.

161

She lay like a piece of limp seaweed on the horse's neck, almost beyond feeling, save for the pain in her foot and the cold in her bones.

She was aware that they had come to the hut, that Muir tied the reins to the verandah rail, lifted her down.

"Not long now," he said, "and you'll be comfortable and dry."

There would be food and fuel in the hut, they both knew that. It was replaced after every lambing. He laid her down on the floor and crossed to the rough table, his fingers numbed with cold, fumbling for the lamp and the matches beside it.

The light was welcome, flooding the cobwebby walls with a soft glow. There was a huge pile of twigs and gum leaves in the fireplace, and logs of *manuka* and pine. They caught alight immediately. Muir lifted Roberta to the dirty sack beside the fire, taking off his waterproof jacket as soon as he laid her down and rolling it inside out for a pillow for her head.

He began to chafe her hands and her cheeks. She opened her eyes in a dazed sort of way and looked at him, then sat up.

"Good." He smiled at her. "Now take it easy, we'll soon have you right."

The lamplight revealed a rough couch at the far end of the hut.

"I'll bring that over here, and get you on to it, as soon as we get you into something dry."

There was an old cardigan hanging on a nail. He took it down.

"This is filthy, but it will do to rub you dry with. We'll have to work fast. I don't want you getting pneumonia."

He brought across one of the blankets from the couch, a grey blanket, indescribably grimy, with bits of horsehair and straw clinging to it.

He turned his back and began peeling off his shirt.

"You can have this, and my singlet."

162

He dropped them beside her. "Now hurry, Roberta. Off with those wet things, rub yourself briskly, and get into these and the blanket. But you must hurry."

"I – I can't," she said, through chattering teeth.

"You can and you will," he said.

Struggling into the singlet, she suddenly began to laugh . . . weakly, but a game laugh.

"In a story," she said, "the heroine would have come to her senses in her own bed, looking as beautiful as a dream in nylon and lace . . . this is just ridiculous. Trust me! Even Burns couldn't get anything romantic out of this!"

Muir picked up the cardigan and began rubbing at her hair.

"Oh, I don't know," he said. "Burns would probably have said: *'O wert thou in the cauld blast, on yonder lea, on yonder lea . . . my singlet to the angry airt, I'd shelter thee . . . I'd shelter thee.'*"

Then they both laughed. She was quite exhausted with her struggles into the singlet, and leaned against him, her face against the bare warmth of his chest. She lifted her head.

"Muir, put that lumber-jacket on again. I don't need it as a pillow now. I'll have one of those old sacks if I want to lean back. You'll get cold."

"I'll get you fixed up first," he said. The colour was coming back into her cheeks now, and the fire was sending out a good heat.

Roberta felt the odour of sweat come up to her from Muir's singlet. Sweat, on a night like this. It had been the odour of fear, fear for her . . . but it didn't matter . . . really. Muir would have searched just as desperately for *anyone* lost in the storm. Nevertheless, it was oddly comforting, not at all unpleasant. When she had lain in the rain and darkness, trapped, there had been nothing to comfort her of human warmth and company.

Muir brought the ancient couch across, draped another blanket over it, and got her on to it, a painful business. She bit her lip so he should not know how he hurt her.

163

He gently as possible removed her shoe and stocking, and examined the foot, feeling her brace herself as he did so. She sat up, and he pushed her gently down again.

"You don't want to look at that," he said. "You've been through a good deal tonight, Roberta. You might keel over."

She was indignant.

"I've never been squeamish, Muir," she said, "and if only Mother and Father had stayed in one place long enough, I'd have taken on nursing. I'd rather see what it really looks like than imagine things."

He allowed her to sit up, and to look.

She said, settling back, in a voice that was purposely steady,

"Oh, well, even at the worst, it's only one foot, and lots of folk make out with two wooden legs."

Her eyes met his with a question in them. He didn't look away. He said, in a voice quite as steady as hers:

"No, you aren't squeamish. You're not a Heatherleigh for nothing. You want me to say what I really think, don't you? It looks a mess, but I'm inclined to think the damage is more to the flesh than structurally. But we'll meet that when it comes. We're only laymen. One thing, you don't appear to have lost much blood."

He ripped some planks off the cupboard door and bound them to her leg to render it immobile, wrapping the foot first with strips torn from the nylon shirt he had bought in Sydney. Roberta had declined to get into it, declaring her struggles with the singlet had exhausted her enough.

The kettle boiled on the fierce fire in no time, and Muir made the tea scalding hot, sweet and strong. He dropped some condensed milk in, making it sweeter than ever. Normally Roberta loathed sweetened tea, but never had anything tasted so good. There was a tin of biscuits, rather stale, but dipped in tea they were delicious. Muir fed them to her. Her own hands were too torn and sore with her frantic efforts to free herself.

He told her of the frantic search that had gone on at

Heatherleigh. Of Meg and Grandy getting home late, having been stranded with engine trouble on the way home, and having to wait a long time at the Maheno garage for repairs.

Then they had got home to find the children alone in the house, terrified out of their wits by the intensity of the storm.

At first they weren't terribly alarmed at Roberta's absence, thinking she must have taken shelter somewhere.

Then later, finding Clancy gone, Grandfather had feared she might have been thrown. From then on, they had organised a search party, men from the whole village turning out, the women trying to trace her by phone, ringing the smithy at Koromiko Creek in case Roberta had gone there to have the mare re-shod, and stayed in the village till the storm spent itself.

They were greatly hampered when some of the telephone wires were brought down with the storm, and men had ridden in all directions to get news of her. Some of the fords were quite impassable.

Meg had kept the fires stoked up, hot water bottles filled, had blankets warmed, feeding the men, and providing hot drinks for them as again and again they returned to find out if there had been any word.

They had been unable to keep Grandy in, they had told Muir. He had begged them not to ask him to stay out of the saddle when his granddaughter was out in the storm. George had got in at ten to join in the search. He had been delayed on the way, as the Wainakarua was over the road, and he had been obliged to make a detour by way of the coast.

At midnight, Andy and Heatherleigh had arrived back to find Clancy at the yard gate, a Clancy with a trailing rein, terrified and trembling. Andy had taken hold of her bridle and led her to the house, where in the blaze of the yard lights he would be able to examine her closely. They were able to tell then that she had been tethered and broken away.

165

That had been the scene that had greeted his eyes as his headlights had swept up the drive, Muir told her. He looked down at her.

"I thought when they said it had been stiflingly hot that you might have gone bathing. I asked Meg to see if your bathing suit was gone, but when she went flying up to see, she saw it was there, on the back of your wardrobe door."

His expression was unreadable. Was he talking just to keep her mind off the pain of her foot?

He continued: "I still wasn't sure — though I said nothing to them." He smiled a little. "Do you remember the day you caught me bathing in the raw? And you said: 'Men have all the fun. Women never dare ... I think it would be delightful to swim unhampered by a suit.' I went first up to Yellowstone Ford. Then here."

Roberta said: "But Muir, I promised you I'd not bathe in the Pool of Darkness!"

His eyes glinted and his lips tightened.

"What guarantee would I have that you would keep that promise? Mightn't you have delighted in defying me?"

She dropped her eyes. He waited for an answer, for a protest, or an agreement. Neither came.

He continued: "I came along by the burn that feeds into this, so didn't notice the *totara* had gone, but on the brae I stepped on to the salmon, and knew you'd been here. Then I found you. . . ."

Roberta looked up. How different it might have been had it been Marie who had been lost in the storm ... this would have been then an overcharged moment when — but Muir had turned his head, listening.

"Ah," he said, "the men! They've seen the light in the hut. Now we can get help speedily."

He strode to the door, throwing it open. It was Andy and Henk's uncle. They came in, drawn and weary, but their fatigue left them as they saw Roberta.

They had a cup of hot tea and some biscuits. It put new life into them.

Muir gave them instructions.

166

"It's not far off daylight, thank goodness. The going would be too rough in the dark, and the hillsides are as treacherous as glass. Get right back to Heatherleigh, get one of the men to go to Maheno ... their lines may not all be down, and ring the doctor at Otepopo, and get him to come at once to Heatherleigh. This foot needs expert attention before she's moved again. They'll need to bring a stretcher, of course. She's warm now, and safe, and she may get some sleep."

When they had gone, Muir replenished the fire, brought a box across and sat beside her. Roberta wondered if he would carry on where he had left off. He didn't. He looked at the small white face, and bade her sleep. He tucked her up gently, slipped an arm about her so that she could be more comfortable, and told her not another word.

Of course Muir would be kind to anyone in distress, from a dog caught in a trap to ... to Roberta, even Roberta whom he despised and disliked. Under her cheek she could feel the strong beat of his heart, the warmth and strength of him. It wouldn't be for long. This would be something to remember, all she would ever have of him. From sheer exhaustion she fell asleep.

Grandy came out with the rescue party, riding George's mount since Muir had his, and the doctor on Clancy. The Reverend Donald Murray was with them too.

Roberta said: "Oh, Grandy, you shouldn't have come. You should have been resting after the wild night I've given you."

The old man bent and kissed her. Roberta felt something wet on her cheek. She smiled up at him mistily.

The doctor's face gave nothing away as he examined her foot and made it more comfortable with what gear he had in his first-aid kit, then he gave her an injection against possible infection.

"I'll see you outside about the transportation, Buchanan," he said. He would have spared old Robert, but

Heatherleigh was not to be gainsaid, and went outside with them too.

The doctor didn't mince words.

"Her foot is badly smashed, but I think it can be repaired, though it will take time. We'll get specialists up from Dunedin. The main thing now is treatment for shock. We'll get her home and rested, then I'll get the ambulance out and get her into Oamaru Hospital this afternoon. She seems exceptionally tough, though she's so slightly built. That examination of mine wasn't easy to bear, but she didn't even flinch."

Grandfather snorted. "Of course she wouldn't flinch," he said impatiently.

The journey through the gullies wasn't pleasant, and several times they had to wait, to ease the going for Roberta. But she was smiling as they came across the great front porch.

Roberta could see that Meg was only keeping back the tears for her sake, but Josephine couldn't control hers at all.

David said unsteadily: "Roberta, I was playing around there the other day. I think I must have loosened the Balancing Stone. I tried to see if I could push it over."

Roberta broke in, laughing. "If it had been set in concrete, David, it would have rolled down the hill when that giant *totara* came over."

David turned and bolted for his room, lest his tears unman him.

A bed was made up for Roberta in one of the downstairs bedrooms, and the doctor took out a hypodermic.

"I want you to have a good sleep now," he said.

She looked up, and saw Muir in the doorway.

"Did I thank you, Muir, for rescuing me?" she asked.

She didn't know what he said in answer to that, because just then the doctor plunged the syringe in, she turned to look at it, then exhaustion, relief, and the drug claimed her, and she sank into the drowsy clouds of induced oblivion.

Three hours later Muir told her she was to go into hospital. She pulled a face.

"I don't mind hospitals one bit, they're the best place when one's ill, but I do hate being away from home at this lovely time of year."

"We'll keep you up to date with progress reports on the changing of the leaves, and the ripening of the fruit," he said.

So he was coming into hospital to see her, then. Evidently you observed a truce in time of trouble! But it would be for Grandy's sake.

Muir said: "George wants to see you. He was milking at Buchanan when you came home, and you were asleep when he got back."

Muir went out, and George came in. He shut the door and came across to Roberta.

"Roberta, when you were out on the hills, lost, I realised to the full how I had begrudged you Heatherleigh. I can only say I'm sorry. I think that in the end I'll go back to my old job in Perth ... as a mechanic. I'll wait till you're recovered. They can do with my help here when they will be dashing in and out to hospital so much."

Roberta's face was radiant.

"God bless the storm," she said.

At Heatherleigh they had some anxious hours about Roberta, but when the surgeons operated, they found the foot wasn't as badly damaged as at first they had feared. Probably the shingle in the river bed had hollowed out enough to take the thickness of her foot, and the water itself would have cushioned it.

She suffered a good deal of pain at first, but gradually it lessened, and she grew stronger again. She was glad of the time in hospital. It seemed like a breathing spell when she needn't plan for the future. It reminded her of weeks spent on board ship when nothing mattered.

Harvest was in full swing on the estates, and Muir was noticeably thinner. He was always thinner during the busy season, he told her, when she remarked on it, and she guessed that the frequent visiting to hospital meant that they all worked harder in between, Meg too. Roberta protested that they visited her too much, that now she was getting better, as long as she had plenty of books she would fill in the hours. Of course she knew that Muir came in so frequently because he didn't like Grandy driving with his heart in the condition it was, and Meg couldn't always come.

One day George brought Grandy in, and stayed after the old man had gone down town to see his solicitors. As soon as the other patients in the four-bed ward were deeply in conversation with their own visitors, George said:

"I'm going back to Perth when you come home. Grandy has bought me a business there. The boss is retiring, he's fairly old."

He paused, and added: "I did Muir an injustice, Roberta. You know that trip he took just before your accident? He was in Sydney on business, and went across to Perth to find out about my work there, on the strength of a suggestion you made to him. It will give me a wonderful start."

Suddenly George flushed. "I've been a bit of a rotter, you know. I was very fond of a girl over there, but – she didn't have a penny either, and I felt I couldn't face married life on a shoestring. But she's always been the one for me."

Roberta put her hand over his. "Thank you for telling me, George. I never took you seriously, you know, when you made love to me. I hope you'll be very happy. There's just one thing . . . never, never let this girl know that money made any difference. Let her just think you couldn't forget her, and realised it."

She lay quietly for a long time after George had gone. It was quite true . . . she had never taken George seriously, but – well, she wondered what it would be like to have no doubts at all about why people cared for you. . . .

She looked up, startled to see Grandy coming in again. It was past visiting hour.

He looked roguish.

"Even if I am eighty, I can still do a line with that Sister," he said. "She let me in for a few moments. Some

170

Spanish grapes have just arrived in Oamaru. They were opening up the cask when I went into Hinton's." He put the box on the white quilt. "Thought you'd like them. Might take you back for a few moments to the time you spent in Spain."

Roberta took his hand and held it for a moment to her cheek.

"You spoil me," she said.

Grandy sat down. They'd probably not turn him out for a few moments yet, and he would take a taxi down to meet George at the National Club. Roberta preferred her visitors one at a time. They gossiped happily about affairs at Heatherleigh.

Grandy suddenly thought of something.

"Muir's told you his news about Marie, of course? Bound to have – he probably told you the night he rescued you."

It seemed to Roberta as if feeling itself was suspended for a moment. As if her pulse stopped, then raced. She swallowed.

"No . . . what news?"

Grandy laughed. "Well, after all this havering about she's landed her Scot at last. Good luck to them both."

Roberta swallowed again. She must find words . . . be ordinary, in fact, casual. . . .

A nurse poked her head in.

"All visitors to be gone, please," she said. Old Robert got up, chuckling, kissed Roberta and was gone.

By night Roberta's temperature was up. The Sister, cool, efficient, kindly, came to her bed.

"Why the sudden rise?" she asked. "We'll have a look at the foot."

There was nothing there to account for it.

"Did you have too many visitors this afternoon?" she asked.

"Possibly," said Roberta, as casually as she could manage. "Some visits excite one more, I suppose."

Roberta had a bad night. So Muir was going to marry

Marie. She needn't be surprised about it, at that. She had always known Muir cared for Marie, and the telegrams had confirmed that. Muir must have given up all idea of winning the heiress of Heatherleigh.

In the wee sma's Roberta felt she couldn't face the idea of continuing at Heatherleigh, close to Marie and Muir, secure in their happiness together. She wouldn't stay . . . she'd cut loose again, and travel.

The night nurse came in. "Are you still awake, Miss O'More?"

Roberta said listlessly: "It doesn't matter."

The nurse thought it did. She brought a bowl and began to wash Roberta, straightened her bed, and gave her a sedative.

When Roberta awoke next morning, sleep had given her courage to face the situation anew . . . whatever the future might demand of her in fortitude and heartache, she wouldn't desert Grandy. He needed her, he was the only person in the world who did. But, oh, Buchanan, Buchanan!

The next day Muir was her only visitor, the first time he had come alone. It might have meant something before yesterday.

He cocked an eyebrow at her as he sat down, reprovingly, it seemed to her.

"I've been talking to the Sister. She says you ran a high temperature last night. Why?"

Roberta's voice held a note of scorn. It had to — he mustn't guess why.

"How should I know? I'm not a medico."

He looked at her sternly.

"Sister thought it was visitors. She told me not to stay too long today." He shot the next question at her. "Did George tell you he was going back to Perth?"

Roberta nodded, brightening. "Yes, isn't it good? Thank you, Muir, for your part in that."

172

His face had never looked more hawklike.

"Then that wasn't what had upset you?"

"Oh, no." Her note of surprise was genuine, but hurriedly, lest he probe further, she added: "What's in that very intriguing parcel, Muir?" She laid a hand upon the package he had laid upon the bed.

"Oh, that." To her relief he left the subject of her temperature, and began unwrapping the parcel. "It's the aerial photos of Buchanan. You remember when they were over? I got the best one mounted and framed. The Heatherleigh ones have come to hand too, but your grandfather wants to show you those himself." He picked up the framed photograph.

But Roberta wasn't looking at it, she was looking at the other picture in the parcel, a photo of Marie . . . the one she had seen in the bedroom, with the shattered glass. It seemed to Roberta as if there was a look of triumph on the lovely pictured face.

She looked up at Muir, praying that her expression was devoid of all feelings she would not want him to read there.

"Oh, I must congratulate you, Muir. I wish you both every happiness in your future life together."

She had hardly ever seen Muir look so astounded.

"What did you say, Roberta? Who — what *are* you talking about?"

This was odd. And it wasn't making it easy for her. Now she would have to put it into words.

"I mean — I mean Grandy told me yesterday about your . . . engagement to her."

There, it was out! And heaven send she had given nothing away.

She looked back to Marie's photo. Muir followed her gaze. His hand took her wrist in a grip that hurt.

"My engagement to *who*?"

"To Marie, of course!"

Muir had forgotten the other women in the ward, and their visitors, evidently. He was speaking in ordinary tones. Roberta was beyond caring too.

173

Muir said, heavy brows drawn together, "Exactly what did Heatherleigh say?"

Roberta started: "He said – he said . . . oh, no, you won't like it, though it was just Grandy's way of saying it. . . ."

Muir's grasp on her wrist tightened till it hurt.

"What did he say, Roberta?"

She looked away from him, and said, unwillingly: "He said: 'Marie has landed her Scot at last' . . . and he said he wished you both luck." She wouldn't, couldn't look at him as she said it. What was the matter with Muir, why was he making her put it into words? If only he knew what it was costing her. . . . She was startled when she heard him laugh. It was a laugh of such genuine merriment.

Then his voice said, close to her pillow: "And to you there's only one Scot in the world, is there, Roberta? Me? I'd like to think so!"

She turned her face back, finding it embarrassingly close to his.

"Roberta, you idiot," he said, and they were the loveliest words in the language. "Marie is married to Neil Cameron, the Reverend Neil Cameron, and is at this moment on the high seas, on her way back to Scotland with him."

Roberta lay back against her pillows.

Muir said hastily, "Are you all right? Am I exciting you?"

"No," she said, "but go on, go on, why didn't someone tell me?" She'd have to gain time to assimilate this piece of news otherwise she would be revealing things she dared not reveal.

Muir suddenly became aware again of the proximity of the other people in the small, modern ward. He dropped his voice to a conversational whisper.

"It's quite a story. Marie played around quite a bit, you know. Anyone as attractive as she is meets with too much admiration. It went to her head. There was no real harm in Marie, only vanity. She was spoilt, delighted in easy conquests, and hadn't a thought in her mind beyond clothes and a good time. Till she met Neil.

"Then she fell in love with someone who wasn't easy at all, who didn't want to fall in love with her. It was right here in Heatherleigh. Marie was staying with her aunt. We had a long vacancy before Donald Murray came, and we had a single minister here on holiday from Scotland supplying at the kirk. There was no doubt he was attracted by her, but he sensibly decided she was no wife for a minister. She wasn't, the way she used to be. He told her he loved her but she would never manage on a minister's salary. That they had nothing in common.

"It hit him hard too. He went back to Scotland sooner than planned. It changed Marie completely. When she knew he had left New Zealand, she thought she would never see him again. Nevertheless, she set herself the task of becoming the sort of person Neil would have liked her to be. It was hard at first, then suddenly she developed a taste for reading and study. Then she took this job at the Home."

Roberta said nothing. She was beyond speech.

Muir continued: "She heard nothing of him for years. He was engaged in work in one of the poorer districts of Glasgow, then suddenly asked for six months' leave, and came out here with the sole idea of looking her up. He had never been able to get her out of his system. He thought she would probably be married; he almost hoped so, but he felt he must see her again.

"He had the deuce of a job tracing her. I'll not weary you with all the details now, but he was almost in despair. Then, quite by chance, he visited the Children's Home with a fellow minister. He couldn't believe it when he saw Marie there."

Muir laughed. "I believe it was quite funny. Neil forgot all about his friend, she forgot all about the watching children, and they simply rushed into each other's arms. They wired me, and I was going up to Wellington anyway. They were married by special licence on the Saturday. I was best man for them. A real story-book ending for two very fine people."

As he paused, Roberta said, automatically: "And you don't mind?"

"Mind – why should I mind? I wanted *you* ... remember?"

She recognised the note in his voice as bitterness, so it gave her courage.

She said, unsteadily: "I thought – I thought you had a soft spot for Marie yourself!"

There! It was out.

Muir stared. "I had a soft spot for her – aye. Because she has been gallant and gay through it all, except for some tough spots I've seen her through ... but if you think I was ever in love with her, the answer is no."

Her eyes fell beneath the intensity of his gaze, and colour ran up into her face.

Muir took an exasperated glance around the room, and found no eyes upon them. He put his hand under the bedclothes, and found her hand.

"Roberta, you've got to tell me, and this is the very devil of a time and place for it ... why did you think that?"

She flushed again, but knew there was no escape.

"This photo here, for instance. I found it in the empty bedroom at Buchanan."

He laughed. "It isn't mine. It's your grandfather's. Marie gave it to him when she nursed him that time. It got broken and your grandfather asked me to get it fixed for him. I shoved it in that empty drawer, and forgot all about it. He reminded me the other day when we discussed getting the aerial photos framed, so I took it in for him. But ... surely you didn't build up a whole romance on that? Or is there something else?"

She said, reluctantly, for this would take some explaining, "New Year's night ... I ran out to ask Marie to dinner. You were the other side of the car. You had an arm about her. You said: 'My dear ... my dear.'"

Muir's tone was quiet and convincing.

"I had rather thoughtlessly wished her a Happy New Year, and she broke down." He paused, grinned, and said:

"I once saw George kissing you. You were completely acquiescent, it seemed to me."

Roberta laughed, and for the first time felt at ease.

"I had to be," she said. "I was holding that Venetian goblet, and daren't break away. It didn't mean a thing."

"You see?" said Muir.

She was suddenly afraid that he might ask her why she had wept later that morning, and that was something Muir Buchanan couldn't explain.

So she said hurriedly: "That necklace you had made for me . . . Marie had a brooch like it . . . and you did fly to Wellington to see her for one day. . . ?"

"I don't know where she got the brooch made. Wellington, I suppose. And didn't you guess why I flew up to Wellington? — To fly home with you. Any other evidence?"

She knew the canoeing conversation could be explained, but —

"Yes. The night of the fire. You had just got home from seeing her, because you brought Henk that present from Marie, yet you must have written her that very night, a huge letter. It positively bulged. I thought no man would write such a letter to a woman at such a time, unless it was a love letter!"

There was pure merriment in his laugh again.

"It wasn't a letter at all. I had told Marie when I saw her that I'd seen a picture of Neil in *The Scotsman*. With it was an article all about his work. Imagine what that would mean to her, when she hadn't as much as a single snapshot of him. She made me promise that the moment I got home I would put it in an envelope and post it to her."

He looked down on her, a smile playing around his mouth.

"Now I'll ask you something. Is this why you turned me down? Is this why you played '*Men were deceivers ever*?' You thought I was playing fast and loose with the two of you? . . . though only the de'il knows why!"

Her voice was only a whisper. He had to bend his head to catch it.

"Nothing else? Nothing else at all?"

Well, she could never confess the other reason ... now she knew Muir didn't love Marie, had never loved her, that ghost was laid. He had laughed about that, because there was no truth in it. She daren't tax him with the other, that couldn't be explained away.

She looked up at him.

"Nothing else," she said. Their eyes met. She had never seen Muir look like this before.

"I could spank you," he said. "All the hours we have had alone, and now I've got to propose to you in a damned hospital ward, with thousands of people around, and the bell due to go any minute."

"Are you proposing to me?" she asked, eyes alight.

"I am," said Muir. "Are you accepting?"

"I am," said Roberta, then the bell went.

In the doorway he turned and looked at her, a long look that plighted their troth as no kiss could ever have done.

Half an hour later a florist's box was delivered at the hospital.

Roberta opened it to find three red roses, dewy-sweet. There was a card in it, and on it, simply, "Burns said it – I'll leave you to guess which poem. You'd better start learning them off by heart if you're to live with me."

Well, she knew that one: *"O my Luve's like a red, red rose ..."* Happiness suddenly flooded over her. Yes, there were still unanswered questions, but perhaps she asked too much of life. Perhaps there were many marriages that had sprung from unworthy motives ... and though Muir had been calculating in planning his wooing, at least she was sure he loved her now. Maybe in time the years would overlay any lingering doubts she might have.

Grandy was pleased, of course, though he shook his head over Roberta when he came in next time.

"Women!" he said. "Even at eighty I don't understand them. It took a landslide and a stay in hospital to make you

178

change your mind!" Then he added, a suspicion of moisture in the old eyes, "There's no one I'd sooner give you to than Muir."

No, thought Roberta ruefully, that's true enough.

It was noticeable that Grandy and Muir were paying very frequent visits to the solicitors just now. Roberta asked no questions. It was better not to delve too deeply. She supposed they were getting things safely tied up.

The specialist called early Tuesday morning, on his way north to an important conference. He pronounced Roberta well enough to go home, and told her that in three months, with reasonable care, her foot should be as good as ever.

Sister said: "Shall I ring Heatherleigh and tell them to come for you this afternoon?"

Roberta's eyes were sparkling. "No, thanks, Sister. I'll take a taxi out and surprise them. I'll go now, and be home before lunch."

CHAPTER TEN

APRIL had come to North Otago. In the folds of the hills the native trees were still green, of course, but on the estate the lombardy poplars were torches of gold and the red oaks and maples were gipsy-bright.

So it was that old Robert Heatherleigh, sitting at his desk, surrounded by papers, was suddenly surprised by two cool hands across his eyes, and a lilting voice saying: "Guess who?"

He didn't need to guess. He pulled the hands away, pushed his chair back, and caught her to him.

"Oh, lassie, to have you back! The place has been like a tomb."

Roberta looked at the mountain of papers.

"Busy, aren't you? Want me to retire? I'll go and find Meg."

Her grandfather shook his head. "She's down the village. I'll ring for Nancy to get you a cup of tea."

While the tea was coming, old Robert tapped the papers he had been busy on.

"These are the blueprints for the Van Wyngens' new house over the river."

"Over the river?" repeated Roberta. "Where?"

"That land Buchanan bought from me. He's letting Van Wyngen have it. We've drawn up a mortgage. Very easy terms. That was what Muir had in mind when he bought it. Did neither of us mention it to you? Now that Gerhard is a New Zealand citizen, Muir thinks he ought to own a bit of the country."

Roberta drew in a deep breath. So Muir hadn't acquired the land for himself. Old Robert noticed nothing. He went on, "I kept the bit with the lime-works on it, of course." He hesitated. "Buchanan and I have been having a lot of discussions lately. I wanted his views on it, and my

180

solicitor's advice before putting a certain proposition to you, but you have the deciding vote.

"I've realised lately what a terrific responsibility a large estate is, what jealousies and heartburnings it can cause. When I allowed Muir to buy his own farm, I got a lot of pleasure, then and since, watching him develop it, putting back more into the land than he takes out, planting out the back hills for future generations.

"I think that the day of the big landowner is gone. In fact, our Government is doing its best to whittle down the big estates, and rightly so. No place for them in a democratic country, though it's taken me a long time to come to that way of thinking. This is a young man's country, and it ought to be."

Roberta sat, her hands clasped in her lap. Once in a while Grandy was quite eloquent.

"Then you came, when life had very little meaning . . . as independent as I was myself. To come to the point, I thought of letting Andy and McGregor buy some land too. I'll help them with the finance. They'll be good stewards of the land. It will still leave Heatherleigh a large property, and it will be yours if you want it, lass, but if you and Muir feel it will be too large a burden, you needn't have it. When I'm finished with this life, I have no right to bind you or Buchanan to my wishes."

Roberta said, unsteadily: "Oh, Grandy, but I know what Heatherleigh has always meant to you, and how you hoped Muir and I, and our children, might carry it on."

The old man smiled.

"Yes, once I dreamed it might go down generation after generation to Dugald's children, and Robert's. But this land wasn't meant to stay in Heatherleigh's name, it seems. Soon Ian and Robert will only be names on the stained-glass windows in the kirk. Most of my treasure is on the other side of eternity, now, Roberta, and I'll not burden you, or Buchanan, with the upkeep of a place like this. Buchanan will be easier to run, and just sometimes, I would like you to remember that it was once part of Heatherleigh.

181

"This house would make a good orphanage. It could be run as a model farm, and be self-supporting, and fatherless boys whose heritage is the land could have the freedom of these acres my lads loved so well."

Roberta was conscious of a mixture of feelings . . . love and admiration for her grandfather uppermost, but under everything, a singing gladness for another reason altogether.

Because this time she must be sure, she said: "Grandy, did you say that you had discussed all this with Muir?"

"Yes. I always do."

"And Muir was . . . is . . . quite agreeable?"

"Aye. In fact, he said he would talk it over with you, when you could do it in privacy, and if you felt as he did, then he thought we should leave Heatherleigh as a legacy to the Presbyterian Church of New Zealand, as a children's home, and the income from the sale of the farm, and the lime-works, could be invested for its upkeep and maintenance."

He looked sharply at Roberta. "But what's the matter, lassie?"

She swallowed before she spoke.

"And – and Muir doesn't mind that my marriage portion will be less?"

She said it naturally, as one might who had lived in France so much.

Old Robert said slowly: "Buchanan is a proud man, a man's man. He'll want to keep his wife himself. He said to me that the only thing that stuck in his crop was the fact that even if Heatherleigh was deeded away, you would still bring him more than he would bring you. What *is* the matter, Roberta?"

She was between tears and laughter.

"Oh, Grandy, what a fool I've been, how unjust! I thought that Muir was after my money. Oh, I know he loves me now, but I thought he had grown to love me *in spite of my money* . . . and I thought you and he had planned it . . . for Heatherleigh's sake."

Robert stared at her, aghast, then spoke to her more sharply than he had ever done.

"Have you taken leave of your senses? *Muir Buchanan!* A man who's so stiffnecked with pride he would take no financial help from me when he set up on his own! A man who was *offered* Heatherleigh a year or two back, with no strings attached, and wouldn't have it!" He uttered a sound of pure scorn.

Roberta was beyond speech. She waited.

He went on, "No, he wouldn't hear of my leaving Heatherleigh to him. It must be yours, he said. Some day you might need it, some day you might come back. How was I to know how you would turn out? If you would grow up with any feeling for the place? I said he could have his name changed to Heatherleigh. That was a wrong thing to do, Roberta. He said, simply: 'My sons will be Buchanans.' He fought to keep Heatherleigh out of George's hands because he realised George was weak."

Roberta said: "Grandy, I eavesdropped on two occasions. Once I ran away, and it looks now as if I would have found out the truth had I stayed to hear all of it. Muir must have meant he wanted the estate to come to me. The second time, I kept on listening, added two and two together and – got five. I realise that now."

She told him all, how she had planned to revenge herself on Muir, had turned him down, had suspected him of dallying with Marie, then, with that cleared up, had consented to marry him, but until now, had not known complete peace of mind.

She expected more scorn. Old Robert's rages could be devastating, she knew. She looked up, caught her grand-father's eye, and he burst out laughing, dropping into his seat and giving way to his mirth.

Roberta didn't laugh till, wiping his eyes, he said: "Very, very like Ishbel. She was aye in a bother about something."

Roberta laughed too, then, and came across to sit on the arm of his chair. She leaned her head against his, and Robert put an arm about her.

"If you need any proof, lassie, last year Muir had his passage booked to revisit Scotland. At least that's what he said at first. Then a week before his sailing date he came to me and said: 'I think I ought to tell you, sir, that if I can trace Roberta, I'm going to. I'll try in the art circles in Sydney, someone should know where they are.' I thought he was doing it for my sake, and asked him not to. I wanted you to come of your own accord if ever you did.

"Then Buchanan said he had always had a fancy to see what sort of a woman you'd grown into. He laughed at himself, and said you might not be glad to see him at that, but he would take the chance."

Roberta was silent from surprise, and shame … and enchantment.

"The next day I took a stroke, a slight one, and Buchanan cancelled his passage. When George turned up, Muir thought he might get away, but we soon found out he was needed more than ever. Of course, if he had gone then, he would have missed you. You were in Auckland."

He looked up at her, on the arm of his chair.

"Never mind, lassie. It would be a dull life without the women, and no granddaughter of Ishbel Mackenzie's could be other than warmhearted, and impetuous, and … very foolish. I prophesy that Buchanan's got a turbulent existence ahead of him – but never a boring one."

Roberta said soberly: "I'll have to make my peace with him. When I accepted him in hospital, he asked me if there was anything else. I made him believe it was only because I thought he was in love with Marie that I turned him down at first … but I think he has always suspected something was wrong." She rose. "I'll go over to Buchanan now."

Robert put out a restraining hand.

"Buchanan is on the road to Dunedin on business. He won't be back till late. They rang for him and he decided to go right away, in case you came home later in the week. He left a note for me to bring into hospital today for you. I'll give it to you. You can live on that till he comes home." He looked at **Roberta**, twinkling. "It's going to do you no harm to wait."

He made Roberta have a good rest in the afternoon, but she persuaded Meg to serve dinner early, and got away to Buchanan soon after. She was afraid that if Muir was early she might have to meet him in front of them all, and she needed desperately to be alone with him.

She wandered around the garden of Buchanan in the twilight, pulling a weed here and there, picking flowers for the vases, planning to plant a golden forsythia in a dark corner, a lilac by the garden seat. It kept her from growing too nervous. Buchanan was a proud man, and she didn't know how he would take this.

When she had the fire lit, and the shades pulled down, she was still nervous and restless. She thought of the other night in this room, when Muir had told her of his ambitions and she had laughed at him. The thought stabbed her. He had been going to read to her from Browning.

She went across to the bookcase and took the volume out. It fell open at the poem that began: "Beautiful Evelyn Hope is dead . . ." and the third verse had some lines underlined with ink, faded and old.

> *And just because I was thrice as old,*
> *And our paths in the world diverged so wide,*
> *Each was nought to each, must I be told?*
> *We were fellow-mortals, nought beside?*

She thought of the young Muir, patiently studying . . . all for the sake of a girl who hadn't been worthy of him. . . . Roberta's eyes filled with tears.

Old Doss sensed her mood, and moved closer, laying her head on Roberta's foot, and rolled over to have her stomach scratched. The old liver-and-white spaniel sighed gustily with content. Roberta's fingers, moving caressingly, encountered an old scar.

She bent closer . . . yes, this then was the puppy that had

185

been caught in the hay-mower all those years ago. Muir had said, not long since: "Doss has had a long life."

If anything could have made Roberta realise Muir's devotion this was it. Grandy had said the puppy must be destroyed. It had happened on her last day at Heatherleigh, and Roberta had wept. Muir must have saved it, but he had not told her since.

So it was that Muir Buchanan came into his drawing-room.

She saw his eyes take it in ... the logs blazing on the hearth, his slippers propped up against the fender, a meal on the table in the corner, the great urns full of golden-bronze chrysanthemums and late asters lighting up the shadowy corners.

"Hullo, sweetheart," he said. "You're home!" The gladness in his voice caught at her heart.

She was wearing the soft brown woollen dress that she had worn the night he talked with her at the old orchard wall, and she was bending over Doss. He caught the gleam of the *paua* shell necklace as she straightened up.

All Roberta's carefully rehearsed speech fled.

She said, irrelevantly, "Muir, this was the puppy that was caught in the hayrake?"

"Aye," he said. "You were so heartbroken over it. I nursed her back to health in the rooms over the stables."

He touched the dog with his foot, gently. Then he looked at her.

"How perfect to come home and find you here. I don't think I've used this room since you turned me down, you wayward wench."

That gave her the opening she wanted. She felt her eyes fill with tears.

"Muir ... I've got to tell you ... I feel this must be explained ... only, only don't be angry with me."

He heard her out, without interruption, to the end of all her stumbling explanations, his face, as always, giving her no indication of his feelings. Roberta awaited his response, tensely.

He smiled, so tenderly that she caught her breath.

"You were afraid, weren't you, Roberta . . . terribly afraid I'd be angry. It took courage to tell me, didn't it? Have you got enough courage for something else?"

"For what?" she asked, wide-eyed.

He laughed. "For the same thing. You needn't suffer any more remorse, my darling. I thought the same thing about you . . . that you had come back only that you might inherit the estate. It hurt, Roberta, because I'd so wanted you to come home. Then, gradually, you disarmed me. I saw how independent you were, how your one thought was for your grandfather's comfort. I still resented the fact that you hadn't come sooner, till your grandfather told me of how you had nursed first your mother, then your father. That his illness had taken every penny you had. That you'd got as far as Auckland and ran out of money, then unexpectedly sold a canvas of your father's, bought your little second-hand car, and came down. You once said to me it made you angry that I was so often right, Roberta. I was wrong, very wrong in this."

She looked at him a smile breaking. He continued:

"So no remorse, my love. One cancels out the other. What do you think of the plans for the estate? Because yours is the final say. You must think it well out."

"I knew the day of the fire," said Roberta clearly, "exactly why I saved Buchanan. It was because Heatherleigh has had its life, but Buchanan's is still to come. This is all I want, Muir, Buchanan, and you. I didn't know it then, but what really brought me back here, after all these years, was the thought of you. How could I know it? . . . a child of twelve doesn't analyse her feelings. I didn't even know I loved you till that morning at the pool, Muir . . . but we always belonged together."

Muir drew her to him, looked down into the green eyes flecked with peaty-brown, and saw no shadow in them any more.

Roberta had come home.

Other titles available this month in the Mills & Boon Classic Series:

BATTLE OF LOVE
by Kathryn Blair

Catherine had two battles to fight: one with her dead husband's father about the upbringing of her son; one with her own feelings for the handsome doctor who kept her stiffly at a distance. A gripping story set on the Côte d'Azur.

AMBER FIVE
by Betty Beaty

Amber Five was the air lane along which flew the aircraft of the Lancing Charter Company, the beam that brought them safely home. And it was a familiar figure to, among others, air stewardesses Sally Matthews and Clare Saunders, Captains Richard Sutherland and Keith Conway, whose stories are told here by an author who herself has first-hand experience of airline life.

THEN SHE FLED ME
by Sara Seale

Sara Riordan had one passionate aim in life, to keep the house and lands of Dun Rury in the family; Mr. Flint, who came there as a paying guest, had also one aim—to escape, from the frustration and bitterness of the past. Could these two people, so different in character but so alike in singleness of mind, possibly interest each other?

35p net each

Available November 1975

Also available this month —
the Mills & Boon 1975 Christmas Pack·

THE DEVIL'S DARLING
by Violet Winspear

'But you don't know me—you don't love me,' Persepha
protested when the magnetic Don Diablo Ezreldo Ruy
announced his intention of marrying her. 'In Mexico,
señorita, the knowing and the loving come after marriage,'
he told her. But would they?

COME THE VINTAGE
by Anne Mather

Ryan's father had left her a half share of his prosperous
vine-growing business, and the other half to a man she had
never heard of, a Frenchman named Alain de Beaunes—
on condition that they married each other. So, for the sake
of the business, they married, neither caring anything for the
other. Where did they go from there?

FLAME OF FATE
by Anne Hampson

It was years since Alana had seen Conon Mavilis, although
she knew he still hated her for having turned him down.
Now, in Greece, they had met again, and Conon, smouldering and embittered, was insisting that she become his wife.
And this time he had the power to make her agree . . .

DARK INTRUDER
by Nerina Hilliard

Young Kerry Derwin didn't want this film unit intruding
into her peaceful, happy life and turning it upside down.
And she wasn't interested in the star, Paul Devron, either.
Certainly she wasn't going to add herself to his long list of
conquests. But then Kerry hadn't yet actually met Paul
Devron . . .

£1.20 per pack

Forthcoming Classics

A COTTAGE IN SPAIN
by Rosalind Brett

Aunt Natalie's legacy of a villa on the Costa Brava was really a thinly-disguised plot to manoeuvre Linda into marrying a charming Spaniard. Linda's English neighbour had charm too; and the situation might have developed as a pleasant, harmless comedy if Maxine had not turned up. For where Maxine went, drama and disaster might easily follow.

THE HOUSE OF SEVEN FOUNTAINS
by Anne Weale

Malaya is the background to this story of a strong-willed girl and an even more strong-willed doctor. From their first meeting he snubbed her and she resented him – but first impressions can often be misleading...

THE RELUCTANT ORPHAN
by Sara Seale

When Julian Dane's first romance went wrong, he said: 'This time... I'll pick my wife out of an orphanage and see that she has no preconceived notions that interfere with mine.' He was as good as his word, but he had not allowed for Jennet's having a personality of her own.

CAME A STRANGER
by Celine Conway

Tess was resigned to the fact that she must give up her hopes for running a guest house by a lake at the foot of the Rockies and go home to England. What she hadn't expected was that when a buyer for her house materialised, he would try to organise her life as well!

35p net each
Available December 1975

Did you miss any of our recent titles in this series?

THE RHYTHM OF FLAMENCO
by Isobel Chace

Lucy went to Jerez to study the Spanish side of her family's sherry business. She learned a lot about the production of sherry – but she didn't think she would ever be able to understand the director, Don Matias Constantino y Mantero.

THE RELUCTANT GUEST
by Rosalind Brett

When Ann Calvert went to spend a month on a South African farm with Theo Borland and his sister, she expected a pleasant holiday; just that. But she got both less and more than she bargained for, including a meeting with Storr Peterson – the most dynamic and disturbing man she had ever met.

CASTLE IN CORSICA
by Anne Weale

Polly Linsey was in an awkward situation—adrift in Cannes, with no friends, no job, and not nearly enough money to get herself home to England. That was why she made the decision that brought her to Corsica as the employee of a total stranger. She had taken a fantastic risk: how would it all work out?

PERCHANCE TO MARRY
by Celine Conway

Marcus Durrant had suggested to Sally Sheppard that she become 'engaged' to him, in an effort to put his beloved grandmother's mind at rest. It was to be purely a temporary measure, with no real feelings on either side – but then Sally found she had fallen seriously in love with him.

35p net each

Did you enjoy this Mills & Boon Classic?

If you did and would like to obtain details of other Mills & Boon romances which are available, or if you are having difficulty in obtaining your Mills & Boon romances from your local bookshop, why not drop us a line and you will receive by return and post free the Mills & Boon magazine – 'Happy Reading'.

Not only does it list nearly 400 Mills & Boon romances, but it also features details of all future publications and special offers.

Just drop us a line at Dept. C, Mills & Boon Reader Service, P.O. Box 236, 14 Sanderstead Road, South Croydon, Surrey CR2 0YG, England.

Will South African & Rhodesian readers please write to P.O. Box 11190, Johannesburg 2000, South Africa. (New titles only available from this address.)